By the Numbers:
A Friendly FFM Ménage Fantasy

by
K.D. West

Stillpoint/Eros

Ebook ISBN 978-1-938808-37-1
Print ISBN 978-1-938808-38-8

version 1.2

Hot titles by K.D. West

See more at:
StillpointEros.com/KDWest

Contents

By the Numbers

Prologue — Null

Jen almost felt as if she might have to thank her best friend for this. Not that Brigid had done anything other than be born on November first. But...

Ooo.

"I think this is why magic was invented," sighed Jen, squeezing Jack tight. Leaving him speechless.

They were fifteen feet up in the air — a simple spell to cast, a tough one to keep going through three rounds of fantastic make-up sex, even with her wand gripped tight. But here they were, slowly orbiting the little chandelier in the empty dorm's lounge. The first two fucks had been properly acrobatic, but this time they were just floating, drifting. Jack was planted deep inside of her, happily letting her do all of the work for once. And all of the work she felt up to was contracting her pussy around that wonderful, familiar cock. One pulse at a time.

Jack didn't seem to mind. Eyes closed. Mouth open. No. He didn't mind.

How many times had they done this? Well, not *this*, because a *flying fuck* wasn't supposed to be an actual thing. Except, obviously, magic. But they'd fucked dozens, hundreds of times over the past year and a half since...

Since.

(Flame and shadows. Smoke and sulphur.)

And yet every time felt like a first time.

She hoped it would always be that way.

Actually, she didn't hope. She just felt. No future. No past. Just *now*.

"Hey, Phalen," she purred, contracting around Jack, "you going to come inside of me?"

He groaned and tried to thrust, but of course that just pushed her away — flying fuck. He whimpered and reached out to pull her to him, but Jen giggled and pulled his hands away from her ass. "No, baby. Let me." She looped her calves behind *his* ass, pulling him back deep into her, and now she answered his groan.

They were late for Brigid's party now for sure — Jen would feel awful later, probably... maybe. Would have to apologize to Bri — and to Tony, which was always kind of weird. Weird that her first boyfriend, who'd been such a hurry to become her first lover, was now her best friend's boyfriend, but so determined to take things slow....

(Brigid's present... have to thank her...)

But now? Now she didn't give a flying fuck. "So," Jen moaned into Jeff's ear as her pussy *squeezed*, "no more sparklies for other girls after this, yes?"

He pulled his face from where it was lodged against her neck. His eyes, so dark that they looked all black, devoured her. "No sparklies. No girls. Only you, Jen Kamiyama. Forever."

Oh, God.... She pulled him deep into her with her legs, and he began to thrust again.

And they tumbled through the air and into each other and into the future.

• •

When they stepped from Outside into the entryway of the Wyvern, Jen and Jack were assaulted by a flood of Metallica music and already-drunk partiers.

"JacknJen!" shouted Rhea Levy, lifting a pitcher of beer that sloshed over her sister Maya's head.

"Dep'ty Jack the Spire-killer!" shouted someone else, and Jen could feel her boyfriend tense up.

She squeezed his hand and stepped in front of him.

Lyndsey Paris and Gabe Sundown — two friends Jen hadn't ever seen quite so plastered — pressed up. Lyndsey yelled in Jen's ear, "So's the birthday girl with y'all?"

Jen blinked at her.

Gabe, usually one of their quietest classmates, bellowed, "Brigid coming?"

Jack's hands closed around Jen's shoulders. "Brigid's not here?"

"She didn't come with Tony?" Jen searched for and found her ex-boyfriend, who was standing over by the bar with his usual partner in crime, Esau Whitworth.

"Tony," Jack barked in that way of his that managed to silence the whole crowd — even with "Enter Sandman" howling over the enchanted speakers — "have you called Bri's house?"

Tony nodded his head. "Didn't answer. Thought she must be with you guys." His coffee-dark skin looked pale — for him, at least. He was hugging a wrapped present — the painting of the four of them that was his present for Brigid. "Worried."

Esau clapped a hand on his friend's shoulder and laughed, "Let's all go see what's taking the guest of honor so fucking long, shall we?"

As if a balloon had broken, the hollering started back up, and everone flooded out the Wyvern's front door.

"To the O'Danan's house!" called Jack, and even drunk, the whole crowd followed his orders, stepping Outside toward Bri's.

1 — Imaginary

"Funny, isn't it?" sighed Jack. "Being here alone."

Snuggling up next to him, Jen nodded. She followed his gaze up to where she had known it would rest: Brigid's picture of herself, Jen, and Jack: Jen's gift to Brigid on her last birthday. Her *previous* birthday.

The first day of every November for the past twenty years, they had come to clean up the O'Danans' house, first just the two of them, Jen's brother Bobby, his wife Morgaine, and Tony, then with some of the greater Kamiyama clan, then with spouses, and children... People had slowly drifted away after a few years — until the previous year, it had been back to just her and Jack, Bobby, Morgaine, and the two last children at home, Bobby and Morgaine's Brendan and Jen and Jack's own youngest, Cynthia. Cynthia Brigid.

Cynthia and Brendan were two months into their first year away at the school now; Cynthia's letters home were still giddy, but they'd already begun to come more and more sporadically.

The Mountain. Would Jen ever think of the school without thinking of it burning? Without thinking of the ridiculous image of Jack facing down Chancellor Spires...?

(Flame and shadows. Smoke and sulphur.)

Morgaine and Bobby had begged off this year — Morgaine had had a conference in Buenos Aires, and Bobby had explained sheepishly that, with the kids all gone now, it was their first chance for a real trip, a second honeymoon, and of course Jen didn't blame them, not after all these years. Even so...

It did seem funny — though not at all amusing — being here with just Jack. All these years, and Jen hadn't noticed it; the steady flood of people laughing and yelling and working had obscured the unutterable *absence*. But all day, as they were renewing the waterproofing charms on the outside of the house or recasting the self-dusting charm that Jen had learned from her mother as a young girl, she had been overwhelmed by the emptiness of the place, by the utter lack of Brigid.

It was only here, lying on Brigid's bed — staring at her own smiling face, Jack's, and Brigid's — that Jen could feel a spark of her girlhood friend's presence.

Jack snuggled up against her, his hand finding the no-longer-taut flesh of her belly. "Jen," he whispered, "It's been twenty years. Maybe it's time —"

"No," Jen said. Definitive as always, though she couldn't ever say why, though she knew that Jack was being reasonable. But even now, after all this time, a part of her *knew*, absolutely, that Brigid was still out there somewhere. Someone so amazing couldn't simply have *died...*

As if reading her thoughts, Jack pulled her closer and whispered into her hair, "We searched everywhere, sweetheart, you know that. That morning. For weeks after. There was no sign, and no sign of her has ever turned up. Even if she'd lost her memory, or if she were hiding, *something* would have turned up."

Jen shivered, but could not answer him. He had heard all of her arguments before, and had happily supported them. But they both knew that those reasons were far from reasonable — were in fact very Brigid-like in their reliance on faith over fact.

"No one believes that Brigid cast the spell that killed her mom. But someone or some*thing* did." Jack's strong fingers, still agile after all these years, stroked her belly as if she were a colicky baby. "And whatever that *thing* was outside of the house —"

" — wasn't Brigid," said Jen. A bloody mass out in the yard, being pecked at by the chickens; Jen had found it when all come up, when Brigid hadn't shown up at the Wyvern for her own party , and the sight, the stench had given her nightmares for years.

Jack sighed. "Probably not. But still —"

She rolled swiftly on top of him and stared down. "One more year."

He peered up at her quizzically.

"If she hasn't turned up by her birthday, next Halloween," — *her fortieth* — "if there isn't some new clue to where she is, we can put the house on the market. And... And put up a headstone for her. One more year."

Jack smiled and caressed her ear with his thumb. "You still miss her, I know."

Jen nodded. It was hard to explain — Brigid and Jen had known each other since Brigid's family moved to Elysium, but when they had all woken up from the nightmare of their twelfth-grade year at the Mountain, it had been Brigid who had held Jen together. As much as Jack had saved Jen — had become her lover, and so much more — Brigid was the one who brought her back to the land of the living. How could anyone so lonely be so loving and lovely? "She was wonderful. She *is.*"

Jack's grin broadened. "She was. She is." He pushed up onto one elbow and kissed her, and for a few minutes, Jen felt very young, and very alive, and very whole.

After some time, Jen leaned up from him, grinning herself down at her husband who was looking very self-satisfied there on the lacy bedspread, embroidered unicorns and phoenixes, eagles and dragons gamboling around his head. "You look pleased with yourself, Phalen."

"Well," Jack answered, "who wouldn't, getting to look up at a sight as beautiful as you?"

"Flatterer," she laughed, pleased. "Want to see more?" Before he could answer or she could stop herself, she pulled the tattered racing jersey she wore for cleaning over her head.

When she could see again, her husband's face was slack, wide-eyed. "Jesus Christ, Jen. What's gotten into you?"

She snorted. "Way to make a woman feel attractive!" She wriggled her bottom against him and was gratified to feel him respond. "Want me to put it back on?"

"No," Jack said, his eyes already narrowing to the predatory gaze that she knew was hers alone. "It's been a while since I've seen you like this."

"Naked?" She popped her bra, releasing the breasts that the years and three children had given her, and wiggled against him again, evoking a soft moan. "You scrubbed my back in the tub last night."

"That's not what I meant," growled Jack, cupping each breast in one long-fingered hand, circling each nipple with a calloused thumb. "Horny as a kid."

She groaned appreciatively as he played with her breasts. "It's the bed," she sighed.

Jack stopped. "The bed?"

Jen felt herself flush and blush. "Brigid and I... We used to lie here. Talking about boys. Talking about you."

His fingers began to explore again. "About me?"

Jen began push up his shirt — like most of his shirts, it identified him: *Federal Bureau of Magic — Marshal.* "She had a huge crush on you, you know."

"No, she didn't."

"Oh, yes, Jack, yes she did." She ran her fingertips around *his* nipples and he shuddered. "We lay on her bed here, just the two of us," — *naked, giggling* — "and talked about you, what it would be like to be with you." *Each girl touching herself, never discussing.* "Her asking me, once you and I were together," Jen murmured, reaching down with the hand that wasn't occupied with Jack's chest and popping the button on his jeans, tugging at his zipper, "what it was like to touch your cock, what it was like to fuck you..."

The cock in question sprang free beneath her. "Can't imagine Brigid ever saying *cock*..." Jack hissed as her fingers closed around his.

"No," admitted Jen, scooting down the bed. "She asked what it was like to have your *penis* in my *vagina*, but she was very fond of the word *fuck*."

She touched her lips to the head of that cock and he groaned, as she had known he would — groaned and grasped the brass headboard.

She gave his cock a good, long lollipop lick and reached for her wand. "Keep your hands there, Jack," she said. His eyes, which had been half shut, sprung wide and met hers. She ran her tongue around Jack's head again. "Trust me."

He nodded. "Always."

Smiling, she cast a spell that bound his hands to the headboard; this much was a game they'd enjoyed before, now and again. "*Umbri,*" she whispered, and a blindfold appeared, covering those dark-on-dark eyes.

"Jen!" he gasped, jumping as she took him into her mouth — the one part of her that hadn't changed since they first got together. "What are you — ? *God!*"

She tugged his jeans down and off, leaving him at her mercy. Removing his cock from her mouth and putting on the breathiest Irish accent she could manage, she sighed, "Jen's not here just now, Jack. It's only me. Brigid."

"J-jen, what — ?"

She pulled her hair free of its ponytail and shook it out, letting the free strands trail up his body. "I told you, Jack," she said, "she's not here. Only me. And you. And your rather erect penis." Her hair flowed over his balls and up his cock, and he gasped. "Oooo," Jen said, still in the more-Irish-than-Irish Brigid voice, "it's just as nice as Jen said."

He panted, his lips working at producing words that did not come.

Grinning, Jen worked her own jeans and sneakers off. "She's said that it's quite nice to fuck you too. She likes fucking you very much." She straddled him, her open, wet sex embracing his erection.

"I like… f-fucking her too!" Jack hissed, and pushed up with his hips, trying vainly to press into her. Jen wasn't ready to give in just yet.

"Hmmm," she hummed, remembering her friend's voice, remembering her calm, lilting tones as she diddled herself, listening to Jen tell her just what sex was like, with Tony, with Jack. "Would you like to fuck me, Jack? Would you like to place that very nice, erect penis inside of me?"

"God, yes!" gasped Jack. "Jen!"

"Brigid," sighed Jen and let her labia run along the length of him.

He groaned deeply. "Okay, okay. Okay."

"Say my name, Jack. I want to make sure that you want me."

"God. God." He bucked and the tip of him just pierced her lips. "Yes. I do. Brigid. Brigid. Please. Let me fuck you, Brigid."

"Oh, Jack," laughed Jen, her pulse racing — it was a challenge to keep her voice soft and airy, to keep her friend's improbable accent — "how nice. I have wanted to fuck you for a very long time."

"I… I've wanted to fuck you. Too. Brigid." Suddenly still, Jack's face darkened. "For a long time."

"Really?" Jen blurted in her own voice.

"Yes. When we were… When J-jen was with Tony." He held his chin rigid, his lips barely moving. "Beat off all the time, thinking of her all the time, but she was with… And sometimes, I thought about you. Brigid. About your hair, about your…"

"My?" prompted Jen, and her breathlessness was less and less an act.

"Breasts. Your breasts. The dress you wore to the Christmas dance you invited me to, showed off your…. Thought about fucking…"

"My breasts?" Trembling, Jen leaned forward so that her own pair, of which she'd never been particularly proud, caressed either of his cheeks.

"*Yes*," he hissed, turning his head to one side and reaching for a nipple with his lips. When Jen pulled back before he could reach it, he groaned, pulling at the headboard. "And you. I wanted… want to fuck, fuck you, *fuck*!"

Grabbing his cock by the base, she pressed down onto him, engulfing him, until his balls pressed against her ass.

"*FUCK!*" he growled, "Jen!"

"Jen's not here," she groaned, not able to keep her own low tone from creeping in. Gently, she lifted herself almost entirely off of him. "Brigid."

"Yes, *Brigid*, fuck! Brigid," Jack said, pushing up so that he was sheathed in her again, "want to fuck you, Brigid, jerked off all of the time, fuck, fucking you, your tits, your *ass...*"

Now it was Jen who was groaning, and there was nothing airy in her voice. The image of Jack fisting himself was one of her own oldest, favorite fantasies, and knowing that he'd done it thinking of Brigid, lovely, lonely Brigid, who had lain on this bed, doing the same thing while thinking of *him...*

"Brigid, fuck, Brigid, fuck," Jack whispered as their bodies fell into a steady, rolling rhythm, pelvis against pelvis.

Jen leaned forward so that her movements and his dragged his pelvis against her clit, and he rewarded himself by capturing at last a bouncing nipple; Jen groaned. An orgasm was bearing down on her, an avalanche of an orgasm, a volcanic eruption, a tidal wave, and she couldn't have escaped its embrace even if she'd wanted to — which she didn't. "Oh, Jack," she sighed, voice airy and breathless once again. "Jack..."

"Dreamed," Jack grunted. "Fucking you... Bri... Jen. Both."

"*Us both?*" Jen howled, ecstatic, and as the orgasm took her, washing her world in light, she saw it — herself and Brigid interlocked, mouth to cunt, while Jack fucked Brigid, and Jen licked at them both. Whether the image came from Jack's head or her own she did not know, nor did she care. She lost herself in the light for a time, and was only brought back to earth when Jack arched up and screamed, his own eruption exploding deep within her.

For a minute or two they lay there panting. Eventually, Jen flopped back off of her lover, her husband. Picking her wand up once more, she released him from the spells that bound him.

Immediately, he wrapped himself around her. Jen knew that some men only wanted to roll over and go to sleep after sex — among others, she knew this from her sister-in-law Morgaine, so the knowledge was all the less welcome.

But Jack loved to cuddle after a good fuck. It was when he was the most vulnerable, the least guarded. It was then that he revealed the Jack that Jen knew that no one else had seen, ever.

Wrapping himself around her, legs and arms, he burrowed into her neck. "Sorry," he said.

"*Sorry?*" laughed Jen, still out of breath.

"Telling you…" He sighed. "I was a kid. They were just…"

"Jack," said Jen, pulling him even closer. "*I* was the one who started the game. Of course you were, of course…" She knew that Jack felt guilt even now that it had taken him so long to reach out to her — felt that it was somehow his fault that she had dated Tony, had lost her virginity to their friend before Jack had managed to get his head out of his ass. His fault that he was so uncertain of living that even during their first months together, he hadn't felt ready for that kind of intimacy.

"Jack, sweetheart," she cooed, "I'm glad. Glad to know you knew how sexy she was. Glad she…" Absurdly, tears seemed to be pushing their way up. "Brigid and I, we… We. She would ask me all of these questions about you, about sex, and you, and…"

She willed him to complete the sentence in his head, to get it, but that wasn't Jack. He lay there, still, silent and patient. It infuriated their children sometimes — as it had infuriated Jen when her mother finished every sentence for Jen.

Jen took a deep breath. "And we — she, but me too — we would, um. Play with ourselves."

That got a reaction. "*Really?*"

"Hmmm. Right here. I thought you'd like that part."

"Did…" His cock jumped against her hip. Jerk-off. "Do girls do that? Together?"

She snorted. "Do boys?"

"No! Not that I know of, at least." She could feel his lips bend into a grin against the side of her head. "Wish I could have seen that!"

"There's a shock!" Jen snorted, pushing him. "You know what I wish?"

"What?"

Again, moist weight pressed up in her throat. "Well, wish she were here, of course. Wish she'd been at our wedding, and the World Flying Championships, she'd have loved that. Knowing the kids. *Having* kids…" She began to cry in earnest. Jack's fingers stroked her chin. "Hell, *sex*. This. She wanted… I wish she *had* got to fuck…"

After a moment, Jack whispered, "You mean, she never did? Not with Tony?"

"No!" laughed Jen through the tears. "Was driving her crazy — well, crazier than usual. She was all for it, but Tony… the poor son of a bitch thought he'd pushed me too fast, and he was trying to do it *right*."

Jack nodded. "He really cared for her."

"Hell of a lot of good it did either of them!" Poor Tony. It had taken him years... Even Esau had given up on him. She shook her head and laughed again. "She used to tell me these elaborate fantasies, how she was going to '*cross the threshold.*'"

"Sounds like she wanted someone to cross *her* threshold, if you ask me," Jack joked quietly.

Jen snorted and swatted him lightly. He had never allowed himself to be much of a twelve-year-old boy, and so on the rare occasions when his adolescent side made an appearance it was always a bit of a shock. "Someone," she giggled, still sniffling. "Tony. Gabe. You." *I want to feel him inside of me,* she'd groaned... "She had this whole idea that it should be like some sort of Druidic rite, which I thought sounded quite kinky. A charmed circle and candles." *A bronze calyx for the blood — earth and metal to contain the power.* The whisper beneath the whisper of Brigid's flesh sliding over her own flesh....

"Out under the stars, probably," Jack said, and Jen could hear an echo of her own love for long-lost, lonely, lovely Brigid. "The Devil's Knob, or the Grey Forest."

"No!" Jen snorted again. "Kinkier and more boring. Down in the basement, *to contain the power released!*"

They both chuckled. "Which basement? At your folks' place?"

"No, silly! Who'd want to *cross the threshold* down with the potatoes and daikon, and Mom's boysenberry jams and apple butter?"

"There's an image. Wouldn't have stopped me, though," Jack said. She swatted him again and they both laughed. "Anywhere with you is paradise. Where then?"

"Here, of course. Silly!"

"But there's no basement here." He sounded bemused.

"Of course there is, Jack, come on." She giggled, and then sighed. "Brigid's dad's workshop."

"Jen," Jack said, slowly. He sat up and peered down at her, his obsidian eyes bright in the fading light of the autumn afternoon. "We've been cleaning this place for twenty years. A whole team of marshals went over this place from the ground up. There wasn't any basement."

Jen sat up. "It... was off-limits." She and Jack stared at each other. "I didn't think..."

Both of them bolted from the bed and scrambled down the circular staircase, Jen naked, Jack in only an old, sweat-damp t-shirt, but each clutching a wand.

They reached the ground floor and Jack began to stalk around, searching for an entrance. Jen tried desperately to remember the one time Brigid had shown her the workshop — it had been right after Mr. O'Danan's death. They had been nine.

Scooting the kitchen table to one side — it had never been so clutter-free when the house had been inhabited — and pulling up a rug, she revealed a circular trapdoor made of flagstone.

"Twenty years," Jack gasped, "and you never *mentioned* — ?"

"*I thought you knew!*" Jen shouted, aware that neither of them was truly angry — that fear and horror that Brigid could have been here all this time... "You said you and the others searched!"

Jack nodded, a grimace twisting his features. "Whitworth cast a *Dezvalui*. I mean, he was always better at summoning than spells, but... There couldn't have been anyone here."

Jen heard the awful comfort in that statement. "Anyone alive."

Jack nodded grimly and reached for the recessed ring. The trapdoor wouldn't budge. After he cast an unsuccessful Unlocking Charm, Jen said, "Maybe there's a password."

Jack frowned, then smirked. "*Cacodaemon*," he said — the sweet-tempered, fanged creatures that only the O'Danans believe existed — and pulled. The door remained frozen. "*Lesser Duh.*" Still nothing.

Jen rested her hand on his shoulder. "Shouldn't we call for backup, Mr. Marshal?"

"Probably." He took a breath. "Do you want to wait, Ms. Journalist?"

"No," said Jen, thinking how ironic it was that she carried that title, which was Brigid's by right. "I want to know."

Jack nodded again.

She nodded back. "It was her father's workshop," Jen pointed out. "*Brigid Elizabeth*," she said, and there was a sigh of released air as the trapdoor popped up slightly. Taking a deep breath, she reached for the ring.

Jack put his hand on hers. "I'll go first; you cover my back." Jen began to argue, and then nodded. He *was* the federal marshal for the territory. After a brief, tight smile, he continued, "Watch for any movement, but don't cast any spells unless something looks threatening — then we stun and run, okay?"

Again Jen nodded.

"Don't touch anything. Stay right behind me—"

"Yes, sir, Mr. Federal Marshal, sir," Jen grumbled.

Jack kissed her. "If she's... If there's anything... difficult to look at, don't feel like you have to. Remember — that room's been closed for twenty years."

Again she nodded, and now she was thinking of Brigid's stories of two-thousand-year-old curses in dark Anasazi tombs. "Yes, sir."

He kissed her again briefly, then stepped to the opposite side of the trapdoor. "Open it on three," he said. "One. Two. Three..."

She raised the door, her wand clutched tight in her free hand. She was only aware that she'd held her breath when nothing happened and she began to breathe again. The open trap was a silent, black void.

"*Ilumina*," Jen whispered, and her wand cast a beam of bright light that illuminated the long set of stairs that she vaguely remembered climbing half-way down with her friend all those years before.

"I told you not to cast anything!" hissed Jack, but when he tried to glare at her, she stuck out her tongue, and he laughed. "Fine, now just watch my back."

"My favorite pastime," Jen muttered, and the glare he gave this time savored more of exasperation than anger. Shaking his head, holding his wand before him, he stepped slowly sideways onto stairs, which creaked, but otherwise held.

The shadows wavered and stretched in her wandlight as she climbed down behind him, making it difficult to make out the space into which they were descending. The near wall glittered, and looking closely she saw a wall full of stoppered phials and jars that reminded her, once again, of her mother's root cellar. Most of them seemed empty, or all but — the contents slowly evaporated over the decades. One or two larger ones seemed to have something floating in them, and Jen looked away, not wanting to see what they contained.

She realized as she looked down that her husband was staring up at her, his lips twisted in a kind of distracted smirk. "What?" she whispered.

"I prefer to watch your front," he said, smiling.

She rolled her eyes. "That's because you and your children gave me a fat ass. Bastard."

"Nope. I like your ass too." Very pleased with himself, he backed away from the foot of the ladder, giving Jen room to step down to the stone floor.

It was cold down here — logically enough. Peering into the corners of the room, she stepped closer to him, warming herself against his back.

"There," he said, and Jen gasped, craning her neck to look around his shoulder.

Just past the center of the room lay a circle of dusty, melted candles, just as Jen had known there would be. Just as Brigid had said she would arrange them, *a circle of flame to protect and contain.*

In their midst, kneeling before the shards of what looked like an enormous, multicolored egg, peering through what seemed to be a magnifying glass, an expression of wonder frozen upon her face, was Brigid.

"Fuck," said Jack, who never swore.

"Fuck," echoed Jen.

As naked as Jack and Jen, Brigid was as white as marble in Jen's wandlight, and as unmoving, and Jen thought she had never seen anything so beautiful.

Or so horrible.

2 —Real

Jen found her fingers reaching out to Brigid's cheek; Jack's hand caught her wrist, and she was doubly surprised — she hadn't been aware of reaching out, and hadn't expected him to stop her. "What? You can't imagine —"

"We don't know what happened. We don't even know for certain if this is her." He was frowning. This was his professional face.

"Oh, come on, Jack, of course it's Brigid. She looks —" Jen stopped and blinked. *She looks so, so, so young....* "— just like herself."

"Still," Jack said, not releasing her arm.

"Come on, Jack, look at her." She could feel dual emotions boiling up, mirroring feelings that she'd struggled with two decades before: sorrow and anger. "It's obvious what happened."

He sighed, peering down at the egg. They were probably as expert as anyone alive at identifying the affects of a Gorgon's stare; between that and the enormous broken shell, it seemed like the obvious conclusion — even if the egg was tie-die colored instead of the the characteristic puke green. "Yeah," Jack conceded. "Poor Brigid."

"Yeah." That summer after sixth grade, lying together in Brigid's bed or Jen's — not diddling together yet, not old enough for that, but poor Bri... "She always wanted to see a Gorgon."

Shuddering, Jack released her. "She wasn't missing anything."

A thought occurred to Jen as she looked at her friend's open, happy, frozen face, and at the blackened lens before it. "Jack?"

"Hmm?"

Stifling again the urge to touch Brigid's cheek, Jen said, "She... She wasn't looking directly at it — she was looking through the lens..."

There was a dull *thump*, and the workshop got darker, quieter. Suddenly, Jen was the one holding Jack's wrist; they were both staring upwards at the blank ceiling. The trapdoor had sealed itself.

"Must be set to close automatically," Jack murmured.

Relaxing her grip on her husband's arm, Jen nodded. "To keep Brigid out when she was little." It hurt, to think of a charm that Mr. O'Danan had set all those years ago still safeguarding a child who had since grown up, but never had the chance to be an adult. She raised her wand and whispered, *"Brigid Elizabeth."* A hairline circle of light appeared in the ceiling; the door had opened again. They weren't trapped.

Staring up at the tiny crack of illumination, Jack mused, "I suppose that explains why the trap was closed. Though not why it was covered."

Jen was about to say that maybe it hadn't been covered, maybe they'd moved the table and rug during one of the annual house cleanings, but realized that if that were so, someone would have seen it when they all headed up to the O'Danan's when Brigid first disappeared. "Hmmm."

"Yeah. Hmmmm. *Ilumina.*" Chewing on his lower lip, he turned slowly, taking in the glass-littered shelves, the table, the empty hearth, the floor — all covered with dust, except for the path of footprints that showed where the two of them had entered. "Listen. I think we should leave, until I can get a team back here."

"I can't leave her," Jen said, recognizing the irrationality of it even as she knew it was true — she couldn't leave Brigid alone in this sad, dark place.

"She's been alone down here for years, Jen, it won't —"

"I can't."

Jack peered into her eyes and nodded. "Okay." Turning back to the frozen figure before them, he said, "Poor Brigid."

"Yeah." The thought that the trapdoor's closing had banished rushed back. Kneeling down, she gazed at the too-perfect sculpture of her friend. "Jack, do you think she could still be...?"

Jack grunted and knelt beside Jen, his gaze, like hers, intent on Brigid's frozen expression of wonder. "Dunno. I don't remember if there's a maximum time span. Don't even think people who're petrified are aware of time — Morgaine wasn't."

"Damn," Jen gasped. She hadn't even thought about whether Brigid might have been aware this whole time. *Poor —*

"Dim your wand," Jack whispered. When Jen cocked her head in question, he extinguished his own.

Still curious, she let the light from her wand die.

Even with the light from the not-quite-sealed trap above, the darkness was as thick and stifling as a Lethifold. Jen was about to ask what Jack was up to when he murmured "*Dezvalui*," and she felt as if something had swooped into the black, enfolding Brigid like an even deeper shadow in the shadow. Then Brigid's silhouette glowed faintly in the darkness.

Jack let out a bark of surprise. "Jesus Christ."

"Does that mean she — ?"

"Dunno," whispered Jack. "But I'd bet so, yeah. Weaker. We wouldn't have noticed it upstairs. But yeah. I think she's in there."

Again emotion flooded up in Jen: relief, grief, astonishment. She felt Jack's arms encircle her, felt him trembling.

They knelt there in the near-complete dark, cold and naked — Jen, at any rate; she could just make out the upper edge of Jack's t-shirt-clad shoulder. Brigid, in whose direction they were both still staring, was utterly invisible.

At length, Jack cleared his throat. "Well, we should get her to St. Anthony's. The petrification recovery team we set up after… And I should get a forensic team out here."

"I won't leave her."

"I know." His lips pressed against her scalp. "I'll need to leave. The phone's been disconnected for years, and with all of the magical interference up at this end of the valley, my cell's useless. You going to be okay?"

She nodded, feeling the roughness of his chin scratching at her forehead. "Let Mom and Dad know we won't be joining them, could you?"

"Sure." His hands ran across her bare back.

"Should probably get my clothes," she mumbled into his neck.

He chuckled. "Probably. I'd rather my deputies didn't get to see this much of you."

"Ashamed?"

"Are you kidding?" he teased back, as she'd known he would. "Wish we could give Brigid the same benefit."

"Doubt she'll be very upset." Jen hugged her husband and laughed. It echoed dully. Amazing how small a room can feel in the dark.

"No? Probably not."

"So," she said, trying to keep the banter light, trying not to think about her friend, turned to stone for two decades, "you finally got to see her breasts. Nice as you thought?"

"Very nice," Jack conceded, "but still not as nice as yours."

"Flatterer."

"Tease."

"Bastard."

"Sweetheart." His lips found her forehead again, and then her nose, her mouth.

Jen felt desire pierce her — the game she and Jack had played earlier seemed to have opened something in each of them; since Cynthia had joined her brothers at the Mountain, they'd fucked more regularly it was true, but never with quite the abandon… They hadn't fucked like that since they were kids. *(Fifteen feet in the air…)* Why was she suddenly ready for him again? *Hungry* for him again? "Jack," she gasped into his lips. Maybe it was just that they finally had the time. But why here? "Jack?"

"Sweetheart?"

Or maybe it was Brigid's appearance, as if summoned by their need. Jen fought the urge to deepen the kiss. "What do you think happened to her? What was she doing with a Gorgon egg, and wouldn't Brigid have protected herself?"

"Dunno," Jack grunted, his lips still against hers. Then he chuckled. "Maybe she wanted to lose her virginity to the thing."

"Not funny, Jack," she said, but still her fingers searched along the valleys of tight muscle beneath his t-shirt.

The ritual circle. *To protect and contain…* She pulled back. "Jack. You don't honestly think —"

"No," he said, his fingers still tangled in her hair. "Brigid was nuts, but no one could ever call her stupid. She can't have known what it was, could she?"

"No." She pressed against him, and his body was warm, and holding him — kissing him — warmed her from the inside as well as the outside. "Have to ask her," she gasped. *When she wakes.*

"Think she'd like to see what she missed upstairs?" murmured Jack, his hand cupping her soft ass.

"Bastard," she giggled again.

"Sweetheart," he whispered, and for a moment she thought maybe that he would, that he would take her right there in the dark before sightless Brigid, in the middle of her dusty circle of guttered candles. His finger slid along her the crack of her butt and between her thighs, caressing her labia from the back, her labia that were still tender from their earlier play. His cock leapt against her belly and her breath caught. Then, slowly, he detached himself. "Later. Okay?" he asked, voice husky.

Where was this coming from? *"Okay."*

He let out a breath and muttered, *"Ilumina."* The light from the tip of his wand seared Jen's eyes. Tears made the glass-filled room flare with stars, and one white moon in its center. "I'll bring your clothes down."

"P-pen and paper?" Jen said.

Jack peered at her, his eyes black and lethal.

"Hey," Jen said, chin lifting, "this is a hell of a scoop. Want to get a quick draft off to Aphra before the Monday morning edition goes to bed. Been a while since I made it off the sports page."

He smiled and nodded, but his eyes were still dark as he stood, then turned and made his way up the stairs.

• •

Once he had brought her the writing implements and her sweaty clothes — the undies moist still with more than sweat — Jack had kissed her again, told her to be careful, told her he'd be back as soon as he got through to whoever was on weekend duty at the FBM — along with a message to Jen's mom and dad that they wouldn't be having dinner together — and disappeared one last time up the ladder, closing the front door to the house with a thud that Jen felt more than heard.

There's a different silence to a house that's got no one else in it. It was a silence that Jen had treasured as a child, since she almost never got to hear it, and one she had been able to indulge in far too infrequently since Eddie, Jon and Cynthia caterwauled their way into Jack and Jen's lives. Caterwauled their way out from between Jen's loins and never stopped caterwauling.

It was a silence that suited Brigid — oddly, perfectly. Even there in Mr. O'Danan's cobwebbed, death-tainted workshop, the toneless tone of the quiet resonated with the peaceful presence of Jen's oldest friend.

Tucking her lit wand behind her ear, Jen laid the paper on the dusty stones by Brigid's knee. Again she found her fingers moving of their own accord toward the fleshlike marble of Brigid's skin. This time, she stopped them on her own.

Could this be anything but Brigid, petrified? Could there be any danger to touching her?

Jen shivered and shook the impulse from her fingers like drops of water. She picked up her battered old transcribing pen, set it on end, took — as always — a slow breath, and began to speak.

"*O'Danan Found.* No. Scratch that." The pen neatly struck out its first scribblings. "*Long-Lost War Hero Found.*" Jen pursed her lips. Still not good, but it would do for now. "Today's date. My byline."

As the pen scratched away, Jen took another breath and looked at Brigid's face. "New paragraph. *Brigid O'Danan, veteran of the Elysium War, was found today, petrified in her...* Hmmm. Scratch to the last comma. *...in her family's house above Sundown Valley, Elysium Territory. She had been missing since her nineteenth birthday, exactly twenty years before.*" In Jen's wandlight, Brigid's face glowed, mouth and huge eyes wide. The darkened lens of the magnifying glass cast a reflected shadow across her throat... "*She was discovered in a secret chamber...*" The word popped out of Jen's mouth before she had a chance to consider them, and left a taste of ash and fear behind. "*...in the house's basement. According to US Marshal Jack Phalen, who fought alongside O'Danan...*" Who had dreamed, Jen thought, of fucking Brigid, of fucking her tits, of fucking Brigid and Jen both, stroking himself there in his bed... "*...she seemed to have been petrified by a Gorgon. O'Danan's mother, Celestina, was found dead on the morning of O'Danan's disappearance. Though it had never been confirmed, the curse that killed him was also consistent with the affects of a Gorgon's stare. The remains of a creature found that day not far from the house may have been that of a newly hatched Gorgon.* New paragraph. *Though it is unclear whether the younger O'Danan may be revived, signs are hopeful that she is, at the very least, still alive. A team...*"

Jen blinked. She remembered Jack talking about the petrification revival team's formation, but couldn't for the life of her remember its make-up. "*...of specialists is attending O'Danan. A group of marshals and investigators from the Federal Bureau of Magic are examining the secret chamber for clues to the origin of the Gorgon.*"

As Jen talked, the tip of her wand bounced slightly, causing the light and the rainbow on Brigid to dance. "*During the war, Brigid O'Danan served as a member and then as a leader of the student resistance movement at the Mountain College for Magic. She fought with distinction at the Battle of the Hall of Mirrors and at the first and second Battles of the Mountain. Before the final battle, she was captured and imprisoned for four months before she was rescued by Jack Phalen...* Scratch back to 'rescued.'" Jack would never let her bring that up, and would only point out… *"At the time of her disappearance she was working as the assistant editor and chief contributor for The Inquirer, a… um, journal of theoretical magic."* Close enough.

"Born in County Connemara, Ireland, she had moved to America's largest magical territory as a girl and graduated with honors from The Mountain College of Magic in 1995. Read back," she muttered, and the pen read the article back to her in its dry, flat voice; she always knew when she'd written well if she could make the story sound interesting even when read in the pen's drone. The article was acceptable; Aphra would find stuff to cut at the bottom, she always did, but Jen had kept it short enough, had dolloped enough exciting stuff in that maybe the *Iris-Intelligencer's* editor-in-chief would leave it alone.

Jen shook her head, and again the diffracted rainbow moved, this time across the white expanse of Brigid's chest. "Oh, Bri. All of the things I want to say in here, and can't. *Her friends have missed her a lot. Or she always made me laugh, even if she didn't always intend to. She had a gorgeous set of yabos that nobody but me ever got to see…"*

A thought occurred to her and she blew out a breath. "Hell. Tony… And Maya. What will they think? What will *you* think?" For a third time, the impulse to touch Brigid's face seized Jen, and this time nothing was there to stop her. Brigid's skin was smooth and cold like the stone that it was, and Jen found her other hand joining the first, found herself trying to rub warmth into the warm, chill, happy face.

"God, Bri, are you in there?" Jen gasped, and felt tears pressing up again. "Can you hear me? We've missed you so much. You've missed so much." One of Jen's denim-clad legs draped itself across Brigid's lap and the other wrapped behind her ass. Jen's arms wound beneath Brigid's, pulling Jen into a tight embrace of the statue. Kissing the cool cheek, blubbering in earnest now, Jen sobbed, "Come back, Brigid. Please come back."

There was a flare of light and Jen squeaked, backing away from Brigid, but it was only the trapdoor opening again. Brigid remained frozen in rapture. Jack skittered down the stairs. "Told you not to touch her," he said.

Squinting at him defiantly, for all that the tears were flowing along her upturned chin, she said, "Nothing happened."

"No," he sighed. "And I don't suppose there'd have been any forensic evidence on her body. Still, she could have had some sort of residual magic on her."

"So you do think it is her?"

He shrugged, then nodded, walking up to Jen, carefully stepping in the tracks that he'd already made. "Talked to the petrification team; they were convinced. When I described the remains you'd found outside, Rhea was sure it was consistent with the body of a newly hatched Gorgon; apparently, everyone knows that the crowing of a rooster is deadly to the things, but no one is quite sure why, what effect it has. She wants me to pull the old files so she can write it up."

"Rhea's on the team?" That was a good thing — she'd been the doctor who'd taken care of some of Jon and Eddie's more unfortunate mistakes. She was one of the best in the country at curse reversal.

"Yeah, her and Gabe. It's the first time they've had a real case to deal with since the team was created, so they're both incredibly excited, aside from the fact that it's Brigid. They'll be up in just a bit, around the same time as the forensics crowd arrive." He knelt and picked up the paper, scanning her article. He was her best and toughest critic; she knew if he thought the article was good, Aphra would approve it. As he read, he nodded, and a knot that she hadn't been aware of in her stomach began to release. Then his eyebrows shot up.

"What?" asked Jen.

"Well," he said, smirking now, "she does have *a gorgeous set of yabos*, definitely, but I'm not sure you want that part in, do you?"

Jumping up and grabbing the paper from her husband, Jen scanned the article. "Oh, Fuck. Forgot to turn the fucking pen off!" She tore the paper neatly at the bottom of the actual article, balled up the other part and shoved it into her jeans. She rolled the article neatly and deposited it in a belt loop.

Jack wrapped her in his arms again. "I've missed her too, sweetheart."

"Yeah," she answered, a small part of her sense of humor resurfacing, "I could tell up in her room."

She could feel his fingers tense, could feel that he was about to tickle her mercilessly — it was no fair that Jack had trained himself as a boy not to be ticklish at all — when the sound of multiple feet sounded on the ceiling, and a voice called out, "Hello? Boss?"

Jack stifled a groan. "Down the trap, Jenkins," he called up. "Mind the step, and be careful where you walk once you're down here."

Jen smirked at her husband, whose eyes promised sure justice — later. Then, together, their eyes traveled to Brigid's kneeling form, and as a half-dozen lit wands began to descend into the workroom, the white figure began to glow like a full moon on a dark, clear night.

· ·

As the marshals began scanning the workroom for whatever arcane clues might still be there, Jen pinched her husband on the ass and ran up the stairs.

"Where you going?" squawked Jack indignantly.

"To file the copy before the morning edition is set!" Jen called back, winking at him. From the top of the stairs, the team seemed to be orbiting Brigid's ritual circle like moonlets; Brigid, still, bright and white, held the point of focus, the center of gravity.

Brigid was not alone.

Jack was with her.

Jen released her anxiety for now — a mother's anxiety? a friend's? — and stepped out into the crisp autumn twilight. Grabbing a tiny apple from one of the trees that grew beside the door to the house — hungry still from the cleaning and the sex — she stepped Outside to file her story with the *Iris-Intelligencer*.

3 — Fractal

When Jen came back to the O'Danan's house — her story filed, Bennet looking actually excited for once — she bounced through the front door in the mood for anything. A good story after a fantastic fuck and finding a friend she had never thought to see again? Fucking fantastic.

What she did not expect to see floating in the house's kitchen was Brigid's pale, still-stony form. Bright golden in the light of the near-setting sun, Brigid shone, her face open, bright and happy as it always was in Jen's memory. The sight made Jen gasp, though she couldn't have said why.

"Oh!" came an answering pant, and Brigid's inert form suddenly dropped towards the open trap.

"HEY!" called a panicked voice from the trap. "Don't drop her on me!"

"Sorry, Rhea!" called Gabe, who was revealed when Brigid's statue started to fall. "But" — he lifted his wand and his bright, bronze face disappeared again — "Jen's here!"

"Oh!" Rhea's face appeared in the trap, just as bright though much paler. "Hey, Jen!"

"Hey!" Jen's eyes flicked back to Brigid's face, her chest — vibrant, golden. "Jack's crew done downstairs?"

"Nah," grunted Gabe as they floated Brigid towards the circular stairs. "But they're done with Brigid here, and we figured we'd get started with her."

"Are you taking her to St. Anthony's?"

"Nah," answered Rhea. Her wand was up and her focus on Brigid, but she was smiling. "Supposed to be better if they wake up in familiar surroundings. So we thought —"

"Her room." Jen felt a thrill of giddy shame at the thought of Brigid's now-debauched bed with its unicorns and phoenixes. Would it still reek of her romp with Jack? Would they know? When she woke — *Please, God, let her wake!* — would Brigid know that Jen had ridden her bound husband sweaty and screaming, all the while pretending herself to be Brigid? "Lend you a hand?"

"Thanks," panted Rhea. Jen pulled her wand from behind her ear and helped the petrification recovery team levitate Brigid up the circular stairs to her room.

· ·

"At least she was inside," Rhea said once they had deposited Brigid on the bed.

Jen blinked.

"Well, most of the worst stories about petrification recovery are because of the effects of weather. Cracks caused by cold or heat. Water wearing grooves, eroding off whole fingers." Rhea shuddered dramatically. "I'm telling you, it could have been a *nightmare.* There's a story about a mundane woman found petrified up in the Rocky Mountains. Been out by a lake for forty years or so — how a Gorgon got up there, no one's ever figured out. She must have seen it reflected in the water. Anyway, they revived her fine, but she had so many bits missing that she bled to death before they could heal her."

Jen looked at Brigid's white perfection, there on her own bed. Not an eyelash seemed to be missing. "So... It hasn't been too long?"

Rhea shook her head, and Jen could have sworn that her nostrils flared. Jen could have sworn just as solemnly that a subtle scent of copulation wafted around Brigid's bed. Rhea looked up at the three faces in the picture on the nightstand and then at Jen. "There've been cases of petrification victims who've been revived decades, centuries later."

"Really?"

Rhea's nostrils flared again, and then she shook her head as if to clear it. "Yeah. One poor son of a bitch was found just after the Second World War in a cave in Kurdistan; he'd been there at least three thousand years. He was revived no problem, but the son of a bitch only spoke a language that had been dead for millennia. Died after a couple of years, and there wasn't anything wrong with him — he was just too lost, living outside of his own time."

"Oh," said Jen, looking at her petrified friend.

"So, Gabe, you're quiet. Caught your breath yet?" Rhea's tone was suddenly very businesslike. "You ready to bring this girl back?"

"Erm," muttered Gabe. He was looking rather fixedly up at the ceiling.

"There a problem?" Rhea seemed genuinely curious. "Come on, Sundown, we've been training for this for five years."

"Erm," Gabe said again. "Yeah. Erm. Could we...?"

"Could we?" Rhea asked. She peered at Gabe and then back up at the ceiling.

"Um. Could we, you know, switch?" Gabe kept looking up; his complexion was rather green.

"*Switch*?" Rhea's eyes flew wide and white. "You want to do the *wandwork*? You hate casting spells! It's — !"

"Um, yeah, just not..." Gabe part his lip and looked to Jen for assistance, but she had none to give — she had no idea what had him in such a state. "Um, not the salve. *Please.*"

"The...?"

"The drills, you see, the victims, they were all..."

Rhea too looked over at Jen, then to Brigid, and then back at Gabe. Suddenly, she gave a loud bray of laughter. "Gabe! Come on! I know for a fact that you've touched a naked girl once or twice!"

"Yeah, well," mumbled Gabe, "They were... I wasn't, you know, *married* at the time."

In spite of herself, in spite of her sympathy for Gabe's abject misery, Jen joined Rhea, laughing for all that she was worth. "I'm pretty sure Lyndsey's said you've touched at least *one* naked girl lately!"

Gabe's face went from sickly (for him) to the color of a salamander in full flame. "*That's just the point,*" he said, his chin lifted in a challenge. "*One* girl, and not..."

"Not... Brigid?" asked Rhea, an elegant eyebrow arched.

"No! It's not that — just the opposite! I..." Gabe screwed his eyes tight. "Look. I can't. Lyndsey... I can't."

Maybe it was her own fantasies bubbling back up, but Jen had a sudden image of Lyndsey and Gabe playing a game not altogether different from the one that she had played with her own husband earlier in the day. "I can do it."

Gabe and Rhea looked at her — Brigid too, her expression no more frozen than theirs.

She shrugged. "If it's just applying some salve —"

"Yes," said Gabe, nodding.

"No," said Rhea. "I mean, it is, but it's in conjunction with the spell that I'm casting, and it's got to be distributed evenly on every exposed surface."

Jen suddenly understood Gabe's discomfort a bit better. "Well," she said, setting her shoulders, "I'm a mom. It's not as if I haven't slathered baby oil all over a baby a thousand times in my life. Sure, I'll do it, if that would help."

Gabe looked at his team partner, eyebrows high. "Please, Rhea. It... I've got some more mandrake, so I could be making up some more of the salve. Just in case."

Rhea rolled her eyes. "Oh, fine. If it's okay with you, Jen, it's fine with me."

Jen nodded.

A smile burst across Gabe's face. He ducked down and drew two wide-mouthed glass jars out of his bag, handing them to Jen.

She took the jars, which were flesh-warm, and placed them on the bed beside Brigid's kneeling form. "So? Rhea?"

Looking down at the bedspread, with its gamboling unicorns and griffons, Jen was sure that she could see a spot right by Brigid's knee — right by the jars of salve. Rhea seemed to be staring at just the same spot. "Rhea? What am I supposed to do? Do I need gloves?"

Rhea stared at Jen, dark eyes wide. Rummaging once again through his bag, Gabe chirped, "Got to be bare skin, actually. Some of the spells require it. Don't worry — the mandrake's actually excellent for skin, one of the best emollients known!"

Rhea grunted, shook her head, and smiled. "Sorry," she said. "Woolgathering." She shook her head again. "So, here's what you need to do: open the jars. I'm going to start casting a series of spells — silent — and you need to begin spreading the salve; we'll start at the top and work our way down. The important thing is that you cover every bit, so don't worry about saving or skimping. Gabe's making more if you need it. And try not to stop — the application needs to be as close to continuous as possible."

"How do I get more salve then?"

"Alternate hands."

"Let me help you get those open," said Gabe, who seemed now to be staring fixedly at Jen's hip. He flicked his wand and the two jars opened, letting out a pungent, bitter scent; the contents were swirling and opalescent. She dipped in a finger; the stuff was thin but viscous, and warm to the touch.

She must have wrinkled her nose, because Rhea laughed; Gabe mumbled, "Yeah, sorry. It's kind of disgusting stuff. I'd have given it a nicer smell, at least, but I didn't think anyone but me was going to be working with it."

"It's all right, Gabe, honestly. I've had my hands in much worse." She looked at Rhea. "Ready whenever you are." *Come back, Bri....*

"Let's go," Rhea said, lifting her wand. "I might still have a date waiting for me at the Wyvern if we can do this right."

"Date?" Gabe said. "Who is it this time?"

"This time?" asked Jen, dipping three fingers into the goopy salve.

"She's never with the same one twice," Gabe said with a smirk. "Young. Old. Men. Women. Jews. Gentiles. Japanese, like you. Indian, like me. Or Indian from India. Or West Indian from the Caribbean. Spell-casters. Mundanes."

"I like variety," grumbled Rhea. "And I see some of them more than once. Sometimes. Come on. Jen."

Jen lifted the liquid handful to the top of Brigid's head and began to spread it along the impossibly fine marble carving of her friend's flyaway hair. Rhea began a complex series of passes with her wand; her dark eyes were suddenly utterly devoid of their usual humor.

As Jen continued to spread the salve, she felt its warmth increase; it seemed to glow as Jen's fingers rubbed it against Brigid's stony head.

What are you thinking, Brigid? Can you feel this? Rhea and Gabe had said that victims of Gorgons didn't remember time passing but —

"Oh!" gasped Gabe. "Look!"

Beneath the pearly sheen of the salve, Brigid's hair, which had been impossibly white just moments before, took on a flame-red hue. "Good sign," grunted Rhea, continuing to cast the spells.

Gooseflesh sped up Jen's arms. Her left hand retrieved another dollop and took over.

They worked on; Rhea continuing what Jen learned soon enough was a sequence of some thirty distinct wand gestures, and Jen continuing to spread the salve, and with it a miraculous wash of Brigid's own coloration.

No movement, however. No softening. No sign of life, aside from the fresh, pink wash of the skin of Brigid's forehead, her ears.

As Jen smoothed the warm, sticky stuff across Brigid's eyebrows and was about to continue along her friend's cheeks — the eyelids were all but invisible, pulled open to their furthest extent — when Gabe whispered, "Eyes too. Don't forget her eyelashes and her eyes."

It was the first queasy moment: running her fingers over areas that couldn't normally have taken the touch. And yet Jen swallowed her unreasoning discomfort and spread the salve across those huge eyeballs; they immediately turned their original other-worldly green, and Jen could not help but gasp.

"Keep going," muttered Rhea, and Jen did, biting her lip to keep the sense of wonder, of panic, of *magic* from overwhelming her.

Jack, who'd grown up knowing about magic only from stories, talked about feeling this, even now: occasional astonishment at it and what it could do. But there was something uncanny about watching the color spread through Brigid's face like one of Tony's paintings.... When Brigid's lips bloomed pink beneath Jen's fingers, the salve giving them both color and the moist, glistening illusion of life, Jen had to grit her teeth to keep from bursting pointlessly into tears. To lean forward and kiss those lips, as if Brigid were Ninianne and Jen the Summer Sorcerer, come to wake her.

As she forced herself to continue along Brigid's chin — she'd never noticed how small and delicate it was — Jen murmured, "So, this date..."

Rhea grunted and started the wand sequence over again.

"...is that what you were woolgathering about?" Jen ran her left palm along Brigid's throat. A flush revealed itself, frozen as it had traveled up Brigid's neck.

"Wool...?" Rhea's wand continued through its dance. She frowned, then snorted. "Oh. No. No, I was... I was thinking about Maya."

"About...?" Jen slathered the salve over an angular shoulder and began to work her way down the arm that was holding the magnifying glass. *Maya. Tony. All those years... Damn.* "Oh."

"Don't think about it, Jen." Rhea's forehead creased as she focused once again on the spells that she was casting. "They'll be fine. It's just... She gets kind of insecure."

"Because of Brigid?" asked Gabe, who was grinding up something pink in a mortar. "But... I mean, I know Tony was a mess —"

For years, Jen thought.

" — but they've been married now forever!"

"And that's supposed to mean she won't get all bent out of shape because her husband's Great Lost Love suddenly returns from the dead?" Rhea grumbled.

"Well, I mean," answered Gabe. "So you're worried Tony is going to throw Maya over? He'd never —"

"Of course he wouldn't," said a warm, smooth voice that caused Jen's nerves to sing. "We're done down below. I've sent the rest of the team home — Jenkins is looking forward to seeing you later, Rhea."

"Hey, Jack. Good for Jenkins — he'll have to wait," answered Rhea, her forehead bright in the refracted twilight. "And Tony, no, he wouldn't. But Maya…"

"…has issues," finished Gabe, nodding, frowning, looking down at his mortar and pestle.

Rhea frowned too, biting her lip.

"Don't we all?" Jen said.

Rhea flashed something like a smile. "Not *you* two. Got all of the issues out of the way long ago."

Jack chuckled. "I suppose. Funny how watching each other nearly die puts everything else in perspective." Jen could feel his gaze on her as she smoothed the salve along one sunken, white armpit.

"I suppose that's true," said Gabe, head tilted. "I mean, Lyndsey watched me get nearly skewered, and I watched her get petrified…." He glanced at Brigid.

They didn't talk about the war much. They all knew what had happened. Knew none of them could ever forget.

After a moment filled only with the sound of Jen slathering salve over her masonry best friend, Gabe shook himself. "I suppose that could be why we've never fought much."

"Nah," said Rhea, her mouth stretched in a full grin, for all that the effort of continuing the spells shown on her face. "It's because the two of you are too fucking *nice*."

"You wouldn't say that," answered Gabe, "if you saw what she and I got up to when she got in last —"

"Yeah," laughed Jack, "that's okay. We'll just have to imagine it. I'm sure it was very…" He grinned and caught Jen's eye; she could see that like her he was thinking of what they had done on Brigid's bed just hours before. "So, Gabe, Eddie blow up the lab yet this year?"

Gabe gave the fond, bland smile that she thought of as his professor face. "No, no, he's doing…Well, not exactly well, but he hasn't had any disasters yet. And Cynthia is proving to be quite as talented as Jonathon."

Jen felt a wash of surprise and shame wash through her; she hadn't even thought to ask after their children.

"Well, it's good that the younger two take after their mother when it comes to potions," Jack said with a smirk. "If they were all like Eddie, you'd have empty… *Sweet Jesus!*"

Jen looked up. Her husband and Gabe both were staring at her, their jaws as open as the flesh attaching them allowed. She realized that her fingers had just swept across Brigid's right breast, leaving the nipple a berry red — very much as bright as Jen remembered it getting at the peak of Brigid's excitement. Jen began to withdraw her hand —

"Don't stop!" Rhea barked, and Jen continued spreading the salve around the inside of Brigid's breast. "Don't want to leave her hanging after all this time, now do we?"

"No," said Jen, her eyes locking on Jack's. "Told you they were nice, didn't I? Like what you see?"

Gabe's eyes snapped back down to his concoction. Jack's remained on Jen's hand, and Brigid's breast, which was turning the same deep pink as the rest of her chest.

Jen brought up a fresh handful of the salve. "Too bad Brigid isn't aware that I'm doing this. She'd enjoy it, I'm sure." Her eyes still locked on Jack, Jen spread the new handful around Brigid's left breast, tweaking the bright nipple for good measure.

Jack's eyes snapped at last up to hers. He smiled.

"Jesus Christ," grunted Rhea. "Can't say that I wouldn't enjoy it myself. Share her with me, will you, Jack?"

"Rhea!" Jen laughed, the spell broken. Her hand passed along the marble ribs beneath Brigid's outstretched marble arm.

"Well, can't blame me, can you? What do say, Jack? Can Jen slather some of that stuff all over me?" Though Rhea's tone was flirtatious, her face had reverted to a mask of focused relaxation.

Jen, who had never thought overmuch about touching other women's breasts, suddenly found herself thinking about how Rhea's pale flesh would look beneath her fingers. *Must be the mandrake. And the fact that I'm sitting here playing with Brigid's yabos on the bed where I played at being Brigid just a few hours ago.*

Jack laughed quietly. "That's not how our marriage works, Rhea. You'll have to ask Jen yourself. I wouldn't presume to tell her what to do."

"Sorry, Rhea," Jen said, watching the color wash along the small of Brigid's back. *Wonder if I blush there?* "Think my hands are going to be done slathering once this one's done. Besides, I wouldn't want to disappoint Jenkins; he's very sweet."

"Screw Jenkins," Rhea said with a snort. Continuing to cast the spells, she flicked her gaze from Jen to Jack and back. "Though I wouldn't want to sow discord among Jack's troops. And mind, that young man looks very nice in a uniform."

A splash of freckles that Jen had quite forgotten about appeared just below Brigid's navel.

"Thanks," said Jack.

"Not that you and your good lady here don't look yummy in your cleaning duds."

Gabe cleared his throat. "Um. Could you stop flirting with them, Rhea? You're making my head spin."

"Fair enough. Can't help myself, I'm afraid. Maya's theory is that I flirt with everything that moves for the same reason that she's such a jealous MacKenzie." Rhea's brow twisted; she started the spell sequence from the beginning once again. Jen felt her fingers flow over Brigid's fluted hip.

Jack stood, leaning against the doorway, one eyebrow showing over his glasses.

"Their dad," said Gabe.

Rhea's wand continued its dance. "Yup."

"Oh." Mr. Levy. Who sided with the Chancellor — and killed Mrs. Levy — during the war. "Oh, Rhea…"

"Personally," Rhea said, "I think that theory's pure crap. I just enjoy flirting, and she's just a jealous twat. Nice watching you do her backside too, Jen, I have to say."

Gabe coughed in something like agreement, while Jack just smiled.

"Thanks," Jen said, working her way down one white thigh. "Hey, Gabe, Eddie sounds quite smitten with the new Summoning teacher, young Tommy's friend."

Again Gabe favored them with his professor smile. "As are most of the male students. She's a lot prettier than old Professor Schuler."

"Not saying much," said Rhea. "And I'm pretty easy to please."

Jack chuckled. "Can't believe he finally retired. Thought he'd never leave his menagerie behind."

"Probably wanted to get out of there before he ran out of digits," said Jen, winking at her husband. Back when they'd been his students, the much-beloved prof had lost three fingers and a toe to various creatures summoned from Outside. At that point, he'd been teaching forty years, so he said he'd have to retire for sure — before his two-hundredth year. Brigid had been one of his favorite students...

Laughing, Gabe lifted another jar of salve onto the bed; a good thing, since the second jar was nearly depleted. "Well, she is *really* pretty, but... How can I put this. Young as she is, I'm not sure that the boys' affections matter to her."

"Are you saying she plays for the other side," asked Rhea, switching wand hands and wiping her brow, "or does she like summoned beasties?"

"She's sure likes them, but the former, I think."

"Which is which?" asked Jack. "Latter and former. I can never remember."

Brigid's flush ran all of the way down her thighs. *Remarkable.* "Former is first. Latter is later."

Jack smiled, watching Jen dab Brigid's knees. "It's a wonderful thing having a writer for a wife."

Jen smiled back. "I live to clear up your grammatical questions."

"Now the flirting is getting to *me*," grumbled Rhea. "Come on, boys, time for you to earn your keep. We need you to tip Brigid on her back so that Jen can get the bottoms of her legs and all that." When Gabe started to quail, she added, "Oh, come on, Sundown. Get a grip. You'll be holding her by her arm. I'm sure Lyndsey won't mind."

As the two men lifted Brigid's form, now fully lifelike but still lifeless, to rest on her back, looking at the ceiling, Jen continued working up her shins. Gabe joined Brigid in staring straight up.

"Once the salve's applied," Jen asked, "how long will it take for her to revive?"

"Oh, if you've covered everything, it should be pretty quick," answered Rhea. "And if you've missed any spots, you just have to keep working till you've got them all."

Jen nodded. Brigid had painted her toes canary yellow. *What a funny thing...* Smoothing the salve along the tops of her friend's feet, Jen slowed. There was only a little left...

"Come on, Jen," Rhea urged, her voice strained. "Just the last part and we're done."

Just like changing Cynthia's diapers. Only Cynthia was my daughter, and she wasn't nineteen at the time. And I didn't have two men and a bisexual woman watching. Releasing the breath she'd been holding, Jen spread the salve through the marble curls, which turned copper as her fingers passed. Pressing on, not giving herself time to think about it any more (*Anything's possible...*) she ran her fingers along Brigid's floral, open labia. Jen couldn't look; her eyes found Jack's instead — Jack's eyes, which penetrated...

Beneath Jen's fingertips, what had been cold stone suddenly became soft and moist and warm.

And a whispy. lilting brogue that Jen had never thought to hear again sighed, "...orgon! Oh! That feels very nice, Jen. What a lovely birthday present! But what are we doing in my room? Why do I smell semen? And Jen? When did your breasts grow?"

4 — Discontinuity

The hours after Brigid's recovery went by in a blur.

Gabe wrapped a conjured blanket around her.

Rhea performed a battery of tests — some that Jen recognized, many that she didn't — muttering incantations, the wand that she ran up Brigid's front and back glowing green, then blue, then purple.

Jen sat, holding Brigid's smooth, thin, warm hand, feeling both young and old, joyous and sad.

When they told Brigid what had happened to her — that she had been petrified for twenty years to the day, that Jen had had three children, which was why her breasts had grown, and that what Brigid was smelling wasn't semen (*at least*, Jen thought, *not mostly*) but the mandrake salve that had released her — she blinked and said, "Oh." Aside from that, she seemed perfectly... herself.

Jack interrogated Brigid gently but persistently, asking and re-asking questions about the night before the attack — the night of Brigid's birthday — and then about the morning that she had been petrified. Very little of the information that Brigid was able to give struck Jen as very useful: she had spent a quiet evening with her mother on the night before her birthday, since the party at the Wyvern had been planned for the following night. "Tonight," Brigid kept saying.

Brigid answered on, blithe and unfussed, more interested, it seemed, in Jen's pen than in anything else. The pen took down Brigid's recollections, which were, of course, eerily fresh.

The egg had been a surprise; it had appeared on the O'Danans' doorstep the next morning. "This morning," Brigid kept saying. "Mum thought it was a Cacodaemon egg, and I thought so too at first; I carried it down to the basement, to show to Tony later. I have it all set up for when he comes over... had it... all set up for when he was going to come over."

Brigid's eyebrows scrunched together, her smooth forehead wrinkling. "Where is Tony?"

She asked this of Jack, who, poor boy, was absolutely unprepared for the question. Gabe too stood, spluttering, his bronze skin darkening. Rhea turned pink — a flush of anxiety or anger, Jen thought, not of embarrassment — and looked to Jen, who took a deep breath, and tried to think how to say what needed to be said. "Tony... He's..."

"Only," Brigid mused, "Mum was in the house, and she was quite old in any case, and so she must be dead, or she would be here or one of you would have said something. Did Tony die as well?"

"No," Jen said, her voice thick; it was easy to remember how amusing Brigid's random insights could be, but easy to forget how disconcerting they were. "No, Brigid, Tony is still fine. He —"

"He's better than fine," interjected Rhea. "He's married. To Maya."

Brigid's seafoam gaze floated from Rhea to Jen to Jack to Gabe, and back to Jen again. "Married?"

Jen nodded.

"To your sister?"

Rhea nodded.

"But..." Her chin quivered. "He is... He... told me last night..." Brigid's smooth, calm face seemed to implode.

Not knowing what else to do, Jen gathered her old friend in her arms.

Jack spoke up. "He held on for the longest of us all, Brigid, waiting for you to show up, to come back. You disappearing, he was an complete mess." This wasn't strictly true, of course — Tony had stopped coming three years before, and Maya had stopped two years before that. Still, it didn't seem worth pointing that out in the moment.

Jack shot a pleading expression, first to Jen, who couldn't think of a thing to say, and then to Rhea, who sighed and, as if she'd have rather have her teeth pulled than speak, said, "Yeah. He was a total fucking mess. For more than ten years. If he hadn't been able to convince himself you were dead, he'd probably have died himself."

"Oh," Brigid said.

"He'll be really glad you're back," said Gabe, sounding far less than certain.

Brigid burrowed into Jen's embrace. "I think not. It is not very pleasant to find that things that you believed yesterday are no longer true today."

• •

The rest of Brigid's debriefing was muted and quick. Rhea pronounced Brigid totally healthy; when Jen asked if she should go to the clinic, Rhea said that it wasn't necessary, and might not be practical, since there was an unusually virulent outbreak of a magical flu filling every available bed at St. Anthony's. Brigid should probably have some company, but she would be fine, either staying there at the O'Danan's, or with someone else. Rhea then said that if she moved fast, she should be able to make her date with Jenkins, gathered up her kit, congratulated Brigid, said goodbye and fairly sprinted down the stairs.

Jen would have bet rather heavily that — whether she ended up on that date with Jack's deputy or not — Rhea was first going to break the news of Brigid's return to her sister and to Tony. Tony, who, Jen knew, would be shattered to find that Brigid had lived after all, and that she had been so near for all of those years.

Gabe stood, a hand reaching out to Brigid, but not quite touching her. "Her bedside manner's never been her strongest point," he joked ineffectively. "Er, I'd love to have you back at our place, but Lyndsey and I, we're in a teacher's apartment, tiny, really, and I'm on rounds tonight...."

"It's all right," Jen said. "She can stay with us. Right, Jack?"

Her husband nodded, and walked over to Gabe, patting him on the shoulder in that bizarrely male not-touching form of embrace. "Or we can stay with her here. Either way. Brigid? That okay?"

"Hmm?" Brigid blinked at them. "Oh, yes. That would be nice." Then she turned in Jen's arms and peered toward the photo on her nightstand.

"It's wonderful to have you back, Brigid," said Gabe, and now he did in fact touch Brigid, stroking her fly-away hair.

"Hmm," said Brigid, still looking at the picture.

"Well," Gabe said, withdrawing his fingers, "I've got to get back up to the Mountain. Lyndsey will be so excited, and Professor Harrington! And... may I tell the children?"

At first, Jen thought Gabe meant all of the students, which seemed a rather odd thing to ask about; Jack, however, understood. "Please," he said. "I know Eddie and Jon will be really glad to hear the news, but Cynthia will be beside herself."

Grinning, Gabe nodded, picked up his bag, said goodbye and made his way down the stairs.

Jen pulled Brigid even closer, as if the feeling of her friend's breathing through the thin blanket might turn out to be an illusion. Brigid did not seem to mind; she simply lay, her head on Jen's shoulder, looking up.

Jack sat at the foot of the bed. Slowly, he reached out, as if hoping not to startle them, and placed one long-fingered hand on either woman's foot.

After a moment, Brigid said, "Cynthia? That was your mother's name, wasn't it, Jack?"

"Yeah," he said. "She's our youngest. Our daughter."

"It is a rather nice name. Cynthia"

"Cynthia," whispered Jen into Brigid's hair. "Cynthia Brigid."

Brigid slowly sat up and looked at Jen, a look of shocked pleasure washing across her face that Jen had only ever seen twice: once after Jen had shown Brigid how to use her wand to diddle herself for the first time, and next on the Valentine's Day before her disappearance when a quarteet of conjured doves had delivered a hand-painted card the size of a mundane traffic sign to Brigid that had, for the first time, proclaimed in black and white his love for her. "Oh," she said. "Oh, Jen. Oh! Oh, Jack!" She threw her arms around their necks, the blanket falling to the bed and dissipating (Gabe's conjurations having always been less than stellar), and pulled them both to her now. "Thank you," she said, crying. "It is nice to know that someone truly did miss me... That you weren't just being nice."

"Of course we missed you!" Jen exclaimed.

Jack threw his arms around them both. "We *all* did, Brigid. Really."

As the hug stretched on, Jen felt as unabashed in her joy as she had in years — since Cynthia's birth, maybe. She embraced and was embraced, and watched sea-changes of emotion flow across Jack's habitually stoic face, felt Brigid's tears against her own cheek.

It was only after they had stayed there for some time that some silly, adolescent part of Jen's brain noticed the bitter odor of the salve in Brigid's hair, which really did smell like cum, and the subtle scent of sex wafting from her own body and Jack's — and maybe the bed itself — and she thought of the fact that they were there, where hours ago they had fucked each other silly, each thinking of a naked Brigid; and now there they were, hugging a naked Brigid.

It seemed surreal.

More than surreal. It seemed *magical*.

5 — Limit

Jack was the first to break the embrace; like Gabe, he was looking down as he stood, not at Jen and unclothed Brigid on the bed.

Is he hard? Jen found herself wondering, and felt herself starting to blush at the thought. *Silly...*

"So," he said, using the brisk, cheerful voice he often took with his marshals and the kids, "Brigid: would you like to stay with us, or here?"

"Here, please," Brigid answered, her head still tucked against Jen's shoulder. "I... don't think I'm ready to leave yet. To see how things have changed."

Now Jack looked up, a frown of compassion on his face. "Right. So, I'll bring back some food — and what else, Jen?"

"Food?" asked Brigid, as if she had never heard of the stuff.

"Yes," Jen answered, stroking her friend's morning-wild hair. "We cleared out the pantry." That had been a painful decision, pushed through by Jen's mom. "A while ago."

"Ah," said Brigid.

Jen pulled her close again and spoke to her husband through a face-full of sunset red. "If you could bring me something to sleep in."

Jack nodded. "Okay."

"And a couple of... Let me write you a list." One arm still around her friend, Jen searched through her jeans' pockets, dumping out some knuts, a cleaning rag and one scrap of paper that had already been written on before finding a receipt she could use. She summoned her pen and wrote a quick list of necessaries — toiletries, as well as some things she thought might be helpful for Brigid. They had kept doses of Insta-Nap ever since the stretch when Cynthia's night terrors had woken the whole family on a nightly basis years before; Cynthia had almost always slept right through, but getting Jon and Eddie back to sleep had been a regular ordeal. She held the list out to her husband, who was smiling at her. "There."

"Thanks. I'll be right back," he said, and left.

Brigid's arms pulled Jen close again. "You're really not leaving?"

"Of course not," Jen answered, and kissed Brigid on the top of her living, warm, semen-scented head. It was... Jen couldn't really have put words to how holding Brigid made her feel.

Whole. Alive.

Jen smiled, feeling the steady expansion and contraction of Brigid's chest within the craddle of her arms. Apparently ten years as a journalist had left her incapable of *not* looking for the right word, even when there patently wasn't one.

"I remember," said Brigid, "when Morgaine Follette was revived our tenth-grade year, everyone in Summoning kept asking her what it had *felt like*, to be petrified for all of those months; we were all so curious, you see."

"I can imagine." She could imagine, too, how Morgaine would have hated the whole thing.

"Hmm. And what she kept saying was that it hadn't felt like anything at all — that she'd been in one place, reading a book... and the next moment, she'd been staring up at Mrs. Skepples in the infirmary, listening to the spring birds singing." Brigid shifted her head beneath Jen's chin and sighed. "I can see what she meant. For me, nothing has really changed: my body still thinks that it is the morning of my nineteenth birthday, not the evening of my thirty-ninth. I am still hungry. Though I am rather tired, which I don't remember being before." She shifted, without breaking Jen's embrace, and peered toward the high window on the west-facing side of her room, opposite the bed; night had truly fallen. "At least," she said, "it is still autumn. It should have been even more confuffling to hear warblers and the catbirds singing. Not that I amn't rather confuffled enough as it is."

"I bet," whispered Jen, rubbing Brigid's back. Brigid shivered. "Should we get you some clothes?"

"Clothes?" asked Brigid, leaning back and gazing that disconcerting gaze at Jen as if Jen were herself crazy. Then she looked down. "Oh. I am naked."

Jen laughed in spite of herself. "Magnificently."

"Thank you. Did it make Jack uncomfortable, do you think?"

"I don't think *uncomfortable* is quite the word I'd use, honestly." The image of his passion-dark face as he'd tried to thrust up into her that afternoon, admitting that he'd beat off to thoughts of Brigid, of her breasts, of Brigid and Jen… "No, not exactly uncomfortable. Gabe, yeah. But Jack… no."

"Oh. Gabe. Yes. He was always rather modest. I asked him to show me his penis once fifth year, just because I wanted to see one, you know, that didn't belong to a Centaur, or a unicorn, or a Hippogriff. He wasn't able to speak to me for weeks after that."

Again, Jen laughed. "Good thing you didn't ask Jack back then. He'd have died at that age." Squeezing Brigid, she stepped off the bed and walked towards the clothes cupboard. "We've kept all of your clothes here. Would you like a dressing gown, or some sweats?"

"Hmm?" Brigid was playing with the pile of detritus from Jen's pocket. She looked up, startled. "Oh. Clothes. Yes. There should some pyjamas on the second shelf."

Jen opened the cupboard; she'd gone through and renewed the anti-dust charms earlier that day. A daisy-yellow set of pyjamas lay neatly folded on the top of a pile; Jen was sure that her mother or Morgaine must have tidied up, since she remembered Brigid's style of putting things away being far less precise. She took the clothes and brought them back to her friend. "Here you go."

Brigid took the pyjamas and pulled them on, all the while staring out the dark window. "I wonder," she mused, "am I not quite twenty, or not quite forty?"

"A part of both, I suppose. Which do you feel?"

Pale green eyes flew wide — wider than usual — and focused more or less entirely on Jen. "I don't know." Brigid stood and walked toward the window.

"Your PJs…!" gasped Jen. Though carefully cared for and locked away from the ravages of light and the elements, the color had faded from the part of the cloth that had been exposed to the air; the pyjamas had a crazy, particolored, harlequin look to them — bright yellow on the arms and legs, with patches of buttercream on the breast and ass.

"Tony gave them to me," sighed Brigid. "For my last birthday." She stroked the cloth absentmindedly with Jen's scrap of paper. "I was looking forward to having him take them off of me tonight."

Jen walked up behind her friend, who stood a good three or four inches taller, even now. She wrapped her arms around Brigid's waist and hugged her from behind.

"It seems odd to me," said Brigid, "that I should be more upset by the fact that Tony will not be coming to fuck me — that he is going to be with his wife — than I am by the thought that my mother is dead. Isn't that rather odd?"

"Not really." Jen found herself swaying slightly, rocking Brigid — whether for her own comfort or for Brigid's she couldn't have said. "It's easier to react to what's more concrete."

"Concrete. Yes." Brigid swayed with Jen and let her head loll from side to side. "Though I suppose I shall grieve them both soon enough."

"I suppose," said Jen. "But don't grieve too much just now, Brigid. It really is quite wonderful that you are back with us."

Brigid turned in Jen's arms, smiling her misty smile, and kissed Jen's nose. "Yes. I suppose it is."

• •

Jack called up from the kitchen as he returned with the supplies from home and a magnificent feast from their favorite Mexican take-out place on Main Street. As the rich scent wafted up the stairs, the color returned to Brigid's face. "Ooo! That smells wonderful!" She all but levitated down the stairs.

"Of course." Jen trotted behind her friend, remembering just how rhapsodically Brigid and her parents would go on about simple rice and bean burritos, which had seemed very exotic to them when they first moved to Elysium. When they were little. When Brigid had parents.

But it was nice to see Brigid's face light up again, to see her smile.

As they ate, and the food's heat flowed through them, Brigid asked about their children, about their lives. "Are you an deputy too, Jen?"

"No!" Jen coughed in surprise.

"Why do you say it that way?" Brigid asked. "I think you would make a wonderful deputy, don't you agree, Jack?"

"Yup," agreed Jack, gulping at the heat of the *buñuelos* that he'd all but swallowed whole — he had a weakness for the corn-and-onion fritters that Jen had always found amusing.

Brigid nodded, looking mildly pleased that she had been right, as always.

"No," Jen said, "I'm actually..." She found herself feeling shy, and only worked out why after a moment. "I'm a journalist. Just as you've always wanted to be. That's why I was taking notes when Rhea and Jack were interviewing you — for me as much as for Jack. I'm going to write a story for *The Iris-Intelligencer*."

"Oh!" Brigid eyes opened shockingly wide. "May I help you?"

"Of course." It seemed so right: who better to write the story of Brigid's resurrection?

Brigid looked from Jen to Jack and back again. "I would never have expected you to do something so boring!"

"Writing isn't *boring*!"

"Well, I suppose not, but certainly it isn't very active. I can't imagine doing something that wasn't about moving about."

"I'm not always moving around!"

Jack grinned. "Yes, you are."

Again, Brigid nodded. "Even when she's sleeping, she's moving. Isn't that right, Jack?"

The grin widened, and he popped another *buñuelo* into his mouth. "Yup."

"I do not!" Jen felt silly fighting the two of them — she felt very much very much ten years old again, with Bobby and Hank ganging up to tease her. *Unfair!*

"Oh, but you do," Brigid said. "Your feet move all night as if you were running, except when you are —"

"Yup. She never stops." Jack jumped in, spraying onion fritter onto the table, clearly trying to derail Brigid; he should have known better.

" — stroking yourself."

Jack grimaced.

Jen stared at the two of them. "Stroking myself?"

"Yes. You stroke your vulva sometimes, and then you stop moving about. Does she still do that, Jack?"

"Yup." He wasn't looking up.

"How nice. And sometimes you pinch your —"

Mortified as she was, Jen looked up to see how Jack had cut Brigid off this time — but he hadn't. Brigid was fishing in the breast pocket of her pyjamas; she seemed to have been surprised to find something there — the scrap of paper. Her nipples were poking through the thin cotton, leaving Jack utterly speechless.

"If I move around so much," she said, "and... yeah, why don't you say anything?"

"Because," Jack said, tearing his eyes away from Brigid's chest and grimacing as he did when he was trying to fight down a blush, "it's... cute."

Jen started to reach out for his hand when Brigid asked suddenly, "What are *yabos*?"

Jen's eyes and Jack's both snapped back to Brigid, who was staring at the piece of paper. The piece of paper that Jen had torn off after the dictation pen had kept taking down Jen's words even though she hadn't meant it to. "Breasts. *Yabos* is a slang term for breasts." Jen stared down at her dinner, poking at a tamele with her fork. *I can't believe I let another person find that! I should have just burned the fucking thing.*

"Oh." Brigid frowned down at the scrap and then at Jen.

"I... I tore that part from the bottom of an article I was putting together about finding you," muttered Jen. "I forgot...."

"Oh," repeated Brigid, looking down at the paper again. "Do you really think that my... yabos are *gorgeous*?"

"Of course they are, Brigid," huffed Jen. "So is the rest of you! *Right, Jack?*"

"Right." Her husband looked ready to crawl under the table.

"Oh," said Brigid. "That's very nice of both of you to say." She picked up some *guisado de pollo* with her fingers, watching the sauce as it flowed from the chicken onto her skin.

Jen looked at Jack, but he shook his head; most likely he was right — nothing that either of them said at this point would help, but more to the point, the whole conversation had gotten just about to the limit of weird that either of them could handle just now. It was amazing how quickly Brigid managed to get you to that awkward place. "You're welcome," Jen said, even as she thought, *It's true.* "And I did play fly competitively, by the way, before the babies made that seem like much less fun. So I *did* move around a bit more — for a while, at least."

"Oh, good. That sounds much more like you."

• •

The rest of the meal passed much more quietly. Brigid seemed thoughtful. Jack had his stoic, mortified look on.

And Jen found herself wondering why she herself was acting so bizarrely. So giddy. So... So *young.* That was it: she was acting as if she had been petrified at the same time as Brigid, and they had both been revived together and Jen hadn't actually spent the last twenty years growing up. Settling down. Forgetting. It made sense. But it was utterly ridiculous.

As they clean up after the meal, Jack gently began to arrange how the night and the next few days would work. "Would you like to sleep in your bed," he asked, "or upstairs?"

Brigid paused from licking mundane ice cream from her fingers. "My own room, please. I am rather fond of it."

"I can understand that," said Jack. "May we sleep in your parents' room?"

"Of course."

"Good. Jen," continued Jack, "I will need to go in tomorrow. There are details of the investigation that I need to be at the Bureau to manage. Can you work from here for the next day or two?"

"That'd be perfect," Jen answered. "It'll be easier to get the article done here — and Brigid can help me, won't you, Brigid?"

"I would love to."

Jack ran a hand through his unruly mop. "Great. And I'll send a pair of marshals out to strengthen all of the wards and keep unwelcome guests out."

Brigid paled. "Unwelcome guests?"

Jen hugged her again. "My colleagues at the paper, he means. No respect for the free press, huh, Phalen?"

"I've got lots of respect for a free press," muttered Jack. "I just don't want to have people wandering around interfering with a crime scene — even if it is a twenty-year-old crime scene — and I especially don't want them bothering the victim, who happens to be a good friend of mine that I'm really happy to have got back."

"Hmm," agreed Brigid.

"Fair enough," granted Jen. "Well, not really, but it means I get an exclusive, and my writing gets to spend some time off of the sports pages, so how can I complain?"

"Oh, Jen," Brigid said very seriously, "if you were unhappy, I am sure that you would complain quite a lot." An odd frown pinched her face. "At least, you would have when you were younger."

"Oh, believe me," said Jack, rising to clear the table, "that part hasn't changed in the slightest."

Brigid looked up. "I'm glad."

• •

After dinner, they retired to Brigid's room again. Brigid wanted to know everything that she had missed. Had climate change made passage to the Cacodaemons' plane more difficult, as her father had predicted? What was it like having children? Was Gabe really teaching at the Mountain?

As the three of them sat on Brigid's bed and talked, Jen found that the past twenty years had taken on an odd unreality; viewed through Brigid's wide eyes — through the lens that her questions provided — it was difficult to see everything that had happened as being quite as real as that warm room, or as Brigid herself, who snuggled against Jen, her head on Jen's shoulder, asking questions and expressing surprise and delight at each answer.

It was as if she had never left.

The children — they still seemed very real. Brigid wanted to know all about them, of course, and listened very quietly as Jen and Jack held forth about their brood: Eddie, who seemed to manage as much mischief as the rest of the family put together; Jon, who had his father's ability to find trouble, but his mother's ability to talk his way out of it; and of course Cindy, their quiet, fierce youngest, who loved animals — of this world and others — and was in the midst of her first year at the Mountain.

"You've told her about me?" asked Brigid, sounding both shy and dubious.

"Of course we have," Jack answered.

"I shouldn't imagine there was very much to tell."

"Don't be silly, Bri!" said Jen. "We told her all about how you and I grew up together, how we went to school together."

"And everyone knows how you fought alongside us," Jack added. "You're remembered as quite a hero."

That brought the memory of the article that Jen had submitted flashing back into her mind.

"Hmm," said Brigid, playing with Jen's hair. "It is rather odd to have shared so much of my life with you, Jen, and yet to find that you've lived so much without me."

Jen found her vision blurring. "Believe me, you were missed."

"Hmm."

They told her about what had happened to their friends — Morgaine's refusal to submit to so patriarchal a role as Bobby's wife, even as she'd happily become the mother of his children as well as the special agent in charge of the Federal Bureau of Magic office in Elysium Territory and Jack's boss; Lyndsey and Gabe's twelve-year-long courtship, their disaster-filled wedding and happy married life; Susan Renyeskaya's invention of the OuterNet, which had brought some of the advantages of mundane information technology to the magical world, and coincidentally made her the richest spellcaster in North America; Felicia Avaya's ascent through the ranks to her current status as the right-hand and heir-apparent of Jill Beauchamp, head of the FBM in Washington; Esau Whitworth's death at the hands of a spirit he'd summoned; Tony's —

The minute Tony's name came up, Brigid became very quiet. When his name came up again, she burrowed into Jen's neck and told them that she had become rather tired. "If you have a sleeping draught, I think I should probably take it and go to bed. Apparently sleeping for twenty years wasn't enough."

Jack handed her the bottle of Insta-Nap. "Good night, Brigid. I'm going to go up and get changed. Jen?"

"I'll be right up."

"Good night, Jack. I am very glad that you found me."

"So are we," he said, smiling and turning up the circular stairs to the master bedroom, which was two stories up.

Brigid shook the bottle and took a swallow. To Jen's surprise, she smiled. "How nice that they haven't change the flavor in all these years."

"Uh, right." Jen had been about to apologize for the taste of the noxious stuff. Jack swore they made all potions as awful as possible so that people wouldn't even consider drinking them for fun.

After tossing back another swig, Brigid said, "My mother used to give this to me after my father died. I've always associated it with that time."

"Oh! I'm so sorry!"

"Don't be. She would come down here and tuck me in, give me a kiss on the nose and tell me how I would never be alone. It is a very happy memory." She downed the last of the potion, put the bottle on her nightstand, pulled back the covers and flowed into the bed. "Mmm. I'm sleepy."

"Good." Jen stroked her friend's face. "You'll never be alone, Brigid." She leaned down and kissed Brigid on the nose; a whiff of the scent of the salve — or maybe of the sex that Jen and Jack had had that afternoon — struck Jen to the core, and she began to pull away.

Before she could, however, Brigid tugged her close, so that Jen all but fell on top of Brigid, and Jen's nipples stiffened further. "I meant what I said," the breathy voice whispered into Jen's ear. "I am glad that you found me — that you and Jack found me. I think I should have been very lonely and sad if it had been anyone else. But as odd as this has all been, it has been rather lovely, to see you. To find out that you are still such lovely people and have done such interesting things, just as I have always thought that you would." Then she yawned.

"Thanks." Flicking the lights off with her wand, Jen stood, crossed her arms, and walked toward the stairs. Uncertain, she turned back.

Brigid spoke before Jen had to decide what to say. "I think your yabos are gorgeous too."

Jen stood there, trying to listen to her heart, to her body — to figure out what she could possibly say, what she *wanted* to say — until she heard a gentle snore from across the room.

"Thank you," she whispered into the dark, and turned once more up the stairs.

6 — Integral

When she arrived up in the elder O'Danans' room, Jack was already lying in bed. "She asleep?"

"Yeah. Out like a light. Actually seemed to like the taste of the stuff, if you can believe that." Jen started to change out of the clothes that she'd been wearing all day — aside from the half-hour or so when she hadn't been wearing anything at all

"From Brigid? Why not." He smiled at her and pulled back the covers, revealing himself to be naked.

Jesus Christ, that did funny things to her too — her breath caught and her middle fluttered, and she felt thirteen years old, not almost forty. "Didn't you bring back PJs for yourself?"

"You know I hate to wear them." It was true. Around the time that they'd first started sleeping together (as opposed to just having sex), he'd discovered that he liked not wearing anything to bed — that besides being (in his opinion) more comfortable, it made him feel less like a schoolboy and less like the orphange product he was.

Unless they had visitors or were in someone else's home. "Jack, this is Brigid's place."

He smirked. "You think she'll care? Besides, she's out for the night."

She rolled her eyes at him. "You just want to show her your junk." When he began to protest, she tossed her undies into his face before sliding in beside him, no more clothed than he was. "Figured you'd got the chance to see hers, so you'd return the favor?"

He tossed the undies over her and into the corner where the rest of their clothes were piled. "Not a chance. My junk is all yours, to do with as you please."

"And don't you forget it." She snuggled up against him. The warm solidity in him stilled some of the wobbles, even as it stirred other reactions. "She told me she thought I had gorgeous yabos too."

"You do," he said, cupping one of the small, flabby chunks of flesh in question in one searching hand. "She's a woman of taste."

"Woman." Taste. Spreading the salve over Brigid's large, white breasts, along her open cunt. *"Barely."*

"Woman enough." He pinched the nipple, teasing a gasp from Jen before moving to the other breast. "By the time you were nineteen, you were very much a woman."

"Or thought I was."

He kissed her ear then, his cock springing up between her legs, and she felt her body, which was already in a state just short of full arousal, slide that last step: quickened pulse, heat flowing outward, a tingling, electric triangle radiating between her nipples and her clit. "Horny," she groaned, squeezing her thighs together around his cock.

"Fucking *fuck…*" groaned Jack, and pulled at her earlobe with his teeth. He began to thrust, and the length of him slid along her lips and between her thighs and sent that current dancing from her clit to her nipples and back.

She hissed and turned away from him, his cock still between her thighs, so that the head poked out from her own pubic hair. She lifted her leg and reached down to guide him in, but his hand stopped her.

They stayed there for a moment, the flare of desire — when had they last fucked twice in a day? — flickering.

Jack sighed, and the flare began to fade. "Weird day."

"Wonderful," said Jen. "But yeah. Weird." She felt his cock soften beneath her hand. "Jack?"

"The deputies I'm sending. You know that's not to keep reporters away, right?" He spooned against her, protective rather than seductive. "At least, not just."

"Yeah. I figured. Not that I mind the exclusive." As he wrapped an arm around her, she pulled it between her breasts. "Whoever gave her that egg twenty years ago might decide to finish the job."

She felt the hot splash of another sigh against her neck. "Be careful tomorrow, okay? Stay with her? Stay in the house if you can?"

"Okay." Jen could feel him relax against her. Funny — all the times that she'd asked him to be careful, and all he'd been able to say in response was *I'll try.*

"Thanks." He kissed her shoulder. They lay there quietly, as they had done so often over the years, waiting for one of the children to go to sleep, or simply enjoying the quiet. After a good five minutes or so, Jack whispered, "I couldn't stand it if anything happened to you. And it would be just unfair for anything to happen to Brigid now."

"Hmm," she agreed, and pulled him closer. "She really is amazing, isn't she?"

"Yup." Jen could feel the puff of the word against her earlobe. Jack's cock, still semi-hard, pulsed lightly against her labia.

"And of course," she said, feeling a ember of that strange, wild spark in her glimmering forth again, "she does have *gorgeous yabos.*"

She could feel the surprised laugh, rather than hear it. "She sure does. Not as gorgeous as yours, of course."

"Liar."

That provoked an audible laugh. Pulling on her shoulder, he slid on top of her, taking her breasts in his hands. "Look at them! They're perfect and beautiful, and they have freckles, and they've fed all three of our children."

She felt the pink rising to her skin, both from pleasure at the compliment — undeserved as it might be — and at newly returning arousal. Pressing her chest up into his hands, she took on the breathy Irish voice from that afternoon. "It is very nice of you to say that you like my yabos, Jack."

He grinned down at her, palming her nipples. "You're very welcome, *Brigid.* I used to have fantasies about them, you know, when we were kids."

"Hmm. Jen told me about the fantasies."

Though he was still grinning, Jack's eyes widened in alarm. "Did you really?"

Now it was Jen's turn to laugh. "No!"

He looked relieved — but almost disappointed.

Jen grinned up at him, taking his hands and pressing them against her breasts even more firmly. "She wasn't quite sure what you wanted to do, though. She said you got distracted before you told her."

"Distracted," he grunted, eyes narrowing. "What do you think I wanted to do with them?" He squeezed her nipples between his outstretched fingers.

She hissed. "I... I don't know," she answered, her voice breathy now all on its own.

"Wanted to see them of course." He released the nipples, and then clamped them tight again.

"Ah! Well, how lovely that you've now had the chance."

"Absolutely. And I wanted to touch them."

"Ah."

"Dreamed about watching Jen touch them. Kiss them."

Why did the image of Jack jacking off to the image of Jen playing with Brigid's breasts make *Jen* feel so hot?

"Used to think about Jen pressing your tits together while..."

"While?" Her voice was barely a whisper now, and high.

"While I... stuck my cock between them." His face was dark now, and Jen knew that he was embarrassed, but that, like her, he was too turned on to care. "I fucked your tits, Brigid, while Jen helped."

Where in God's name had sixteen-year-old Jack got an image like *that*? Some magazine? No access to internet porn for magical kids then. Some guy's boast? *If he'd told me then, would it have made me as horny as it does right now?* "I... Jen is holding my breasts together now, Jack." She was, too. "Would you like to fuck them?"

He grunted, looking down at her with that predator's intensity that always turned her to mush.

"Please, Jack," she said, before realizing that she had dropped her Brigid voice. "Please fuck Brigid's tits."

"Never could refuse you," he growled. She could feel his cock jump, rock-hard, against her sternum. Letting go of her hands he grabbed the heavy oak headboard and scooted forward, pressing his cock into the valley of flesh between her breasts.

Morgaine had talked to her about doing this, of course, during her time of the month, since oral sex with Bobby was out of the question given the relative size of things Jen really didn't want to think about, either in that moment, feeling Jack's cock spreading her tits, feeling his hips roll against her nipples, nor when Jen and her sister-in-law had discussed it after several bottles of wine. Morgaine had said that she and Bobby had both enjoyed it, and Jen could see why: it felt nice, yeah, though nothing special, but there was something amazing about feeling the heat of him piercing her in a way that was so new yet so familiarly intimate, even as she was able to stare up at him and watch the affect that her body was having on him.

Ah, well. When she and Morgaine had had that drunken giggle-fest back after Jen's first season racing, Jen'd had even less to press together than she had now, while Morgaine had had plenty. *Not as much as Brigid, of course....*

And, of course, since the very beginning, giving and receiving oral sex had been a favorite part of Jen and Jack's sexual routine.

Sexual this day may be, but it's anything but routine.

Precum from Jack's cock was beginning to slicken the insides of Jen's breasts and dab the underside of her chin. His eyes had begun to drift closed. "D'you know, Jack," Jen trilled in her Brigid voice, "Jen has always said that it was very nice to take that lovely penis of yours in her mouth. I wonder…"

As he withdrew, she looked down to where his cock was nestled and realized, *Yes, this will be lovely indeed.* As the head of his cock, dark and glistening, pressed up from between her tits, she opened her mouth and welcomed it against her tongue, giving the tip a flick as it began to withdraw again.

"*Brigid!*" moaned Jack, and Jen felt tickled that he didn't need to be reminded of the game, even as a small prick of jealousy jabbed at her, and yet Brigid's presence — her *real* presence, her presence as an *idea* — filled Jen with a feeling, so much feeling that she felt herself overflowing, inside and out, and *she* was moaning, *screaming,* wordless, and wet heat flowed down and *up,* and Jack was coming, into her mouth, onto her neck, and *Brigid…*

And Jack was kissing her, panting, lying atop her. "*Jesus.*" He kissed her cheeks, her neck, her chin, her mouth, everywhere that there his jism had flowed, and then his mouth found hers, and the taste of him in his own, like liquor.

His wet cock pressed against her belly, still streaming, and she could feel him soft, but knew her need and knew that he could meet it. "Eat me," she whispered, panted, "eat me, eat me."

He stilled atop her for a moment, and she wondered what she had said to break the mood, because — *oh!* — she was still in the mood, when he moved atop her and whispered back, "Do you trust me?"

"Always. With my life." It was not anything that she had ever said to him: it was something she would have felt too silly to say when they were young and had never felt the need to say in later years. Yet it was true, and she hoped that he had always known it.

His mouth found hers again. He whispered again: "Put your hands up above your head."

She did, and was not shocked when he bound them to the cornerposts of the big bed. "*Umbri,*" he murmured, and her vision darkened.

"*Jack?*" she groaned — frightened even though she knew that he meant her nothing but good.

A breathy, hoarse attempt at a brogue answered her, "Jack's gone, Jen. He asked me to take care of you."

The voice was such a ridiculous put-on that she almost burst out laughing; the reversal of her own game, however, was so sweet, and the fantasy so close to the half-submerged images that she'd been trying not to look at since this afternoon that she found herself gasping, "*Brigid?*"

"Yes," answered breathy falsetto.

She did laugh now, and she hoped that Jack knew her well enough to know how delighted she felt. "How nice!"

"I think so too."

His body moved off of hers. She reached for him with her lips, her legs, but he was out of her reach. "And… how are you going to, er, *take care* of me?"

No answer came, but suddenly a wet heat surrounded the big toe of her left foot, and *oooooooohh…*

She had always wondered what Jack felt like when she took him in her mouth. Maybe she didn't know now, but she definitely had an idea…

Unbidden, the image sprang to her mind of a red head bent over her foot rather than a black one, and if anything, the image made her cunt flower further. "God, Jack, Jack, please!"

"Jack isn't here, Jen. It's just me."

Again the impulse to laugh bubbled up, but lips found her ankle and a tongue began to trace its way up the inside of her calf; laughter melted into a moan. "*Brigid…*"

"Yes," came a hissed answer, followed by another murmer, and then Jen thought she felt the susurrus of hair flowing over her thigh, and she let out another cry: "*Brigid!*"

And then fingers found her lips and squeezed and she was wordless and thoughtless, and a tongue touched her clit…

Jen had discovered masturbation so young that she couldn't remember a time when she hadn't played with herself. When Bobby and Jen's oldest brother Hank had tried to tell her it wasn't polite, she'd been maybe seven, and had told him that he was being silly, that she'd seen him doing it three times that day, so in future he could remember to close his own door and to knock before entering hers, but she'd do what she wanted in her own room.

But the first time that she could remember having an orgasm — a real time-stopping, toe-curling orgasm — was late one night at Brigid's, sitting on her bed. It must have been just before ninth grade, because Jen had been telling Brigid about spying on Hank one night when he'd snuck of with some girl who was camping in the woods — actually, spying on the girl, because Hank had been lying on his back, out of sight, and she'd been just barely visible through the flap of her tent, kneeling astride him, pinching at her nipples, screaming in a language Jen couldn't even guess at. French, maybe? Jen had never heard French then.

And after Jen had finished the story, the two of them had lain there, pinching at their own nipples, and Jen had started to giggle, because, actually, it felt really *good*, and then Brigid had begun to ask about Jack — she often did when they did this — and Jen had said that she'd really like to introduce Brigid to Jack. After all, Jen was seeing Michael — why shouldn't Jack fall in love with Brigid? And Brigid, pinching her tits berry-bright, had gone all pink and said no one would fall in love with her, but Jen had told her she was being silly — Brigid was lovely and loveable, and Jack was sure to fall in love with her, and then Brigid would be the one sitting astride Jack, pinching her nipples and moaning.

And Brigid had moaned.

And Jen had seen it as clearly as the memory of Hank with the foreign girl out in the Grey Forest: Brigid fucking Jack. Clearer. And she'd wanted it. Wanted them to fuck. Wanted to watch them fuck. And in her mind then, *she* was Brigid, and the fingers in her cunt Jack, and she screamed as Brigid's mouth whipped hot against her clit and her fingers lit a flame inside that screamed *BrigidBrigidBrigid!*

And Jen was weeping beneath her spell-cast blindfold, her chest heaving and her cunt pulsing around fingers that Jen knew to be Jack's but was sure were her oldest, new-found friend's.

"I love you too, Jen," said Brigid's true voice from the foot of the bed. "And Jen was right, Jack. You have a very nice penis."

7 — Convergence

"Did I say something?" asked Brigid, as Jack withdrew his mouth and hand from Jen's cunt and dove off of the bed — spell-blinded as she was, Jen had to assume that he was diving toward the pile of clothing that they'd left in the corner.

"Brigid!" was all that Jen could think to say; she was deeply embarrassed, but also coming down off of an orgasm that had left her feeling as if half of her bones might have been vanished. Some part of her body clearly opted for modesty and tried to cover her nakedness, but of course her hands were bound to the headboard and so she lay there, splayed open like shucked oyster.

"Yes, you said my name quite loudly before, too," said Brigid, very quietly. Jen could feel her friend sit on the end of the bed; she tried to pull her knees up to cover herself, but realized that that simply exposed her pussy, and so she gave it up as a bad job and let her legs flop bonelessly open once again. Brigid continued, "That was what woke me."

"We're *so* sorry we woke you, Brigid," whimpered Jack. There was a loud thump, followed by a grunt; Jen got the impression that he'd fallen over while trying to pull his jeans on.

"Oh, don't be sorry," Brigid said. "I'd been having a rather disturbing dream about eggs with eyes, and then I heard my name, and I found myself up here, and you were having sex in a way I've never considered and Jen was saying my name and having what looked to be a rather remarkable orgasm, and she said that she loved me, which was very nice, and all in all it was the most beautiful thing I've ever seen. Thank you." Brigid's voice had a liquid sound to it that Jen didn't recognize.

"Um, you're welcome," said Jen, squirming. *Loved…?* "But Brigid —"

A featherlight touch brushed the inside of Jen's leg, and she froze. She wanted to ask — to *tell* Brigid to stop, or maybe to move just a *little* further up, but she found that all of her muscles had frozen, like a faun's at the sight of a coyote.

"Beautiful," whispered Brigid, and Jen heard Jack gasp, and felt long hair brush her thighs, and then a tongue ran up the length of her lips and —

If the orgasm that Jack had lit in Jen had gone off like a bonfire, smoldering from the inside until the whole of her suddenly exploded into flame, then this was like a celestial version of the annual Fourth of July fireworks: out of darkness, infinite light.

When Jen's hearing cleared, she heard what might have been an echo: Brigid's voice whispering again. "Beautiful."

Jen could think of nothing to add.

"Listen, Brigid —" Jack began.

"Oh, Jack, don't feel as if you have to get dressed again. Jen has told me that you like to sleep in the nude. I do myself. And I've already seen you, so there's no need to be bashful."

"Uh…"

"Look, I'll take mine off too. That way it's simpler. I find that other people wearing clothing makes me feel more naked."

Some distant part of Jen's mind actually found itself thinking that that made sense. Which it did, in a very Brigid sort of way. Though how one could be more naked than naked…

Jack, however, didn't seem to be buying. "Look, Brigid —"

Jen heard the harlequin-colored pyjamas hit the bed — felt cotton drape over one of her own limp feet.

Jack was silent.

Jen was beyond. "Brigid. I think you're scaring Jack. I'd be terrified that you'd walked in on us screaming your name while fucking if I hadn't just had two brain-scrambling trips out of my body in the last five minutes."

"Oh," said Brigid, sounding quite contrite. "I didn't mean to frighten you. In all honesty, I didn't think it was possible. You are the two bravest people I know."

"Thanks," Jack said, polite boy that he was.

"Speaking of which," said Jen, "brave though I may be, and as much as I'm enjoying lying here —"

"Oh!" Jack released her with a quick flick of his wand.

When Jen's vision cleared, the first thing that she saw was the PJs draped over her toes, and Brigid's hands, mothing at the buttercream cotton. Looking up, she saw two breasts — breasts that she had seen a lot more of today than she ever could have imagined — and of course those two green eyes, focused, as Jen had known they would be, directly on her.

Jen pulled her knees to her own chest, very aware that it was pointless. "So. Bad dream about eggs with eyes?" She reached out with both hands.

Brigid folded herself into them, resting her head on Jen's knees, soft breasts against hard shins. "Yes. Having bad dreams can be very interesting sometimes, but not when they're boring and obvious."

"I know what you mean," muttered Jack, who hadn't had a bad dream that Jen knew of in years.

"Hmm," agreed Brigid.

Jen stroked her friend's wild hair, which was softer than Jen remembered. "Happy birthday."

"Hmm."

Jack sat on the side of the bed. Jen watched him stifle the urge to reach out and touch Brigid's arm, and so she did it for him, stroking the white miracle of it — still like marble and yet soft and *warm*.... His eyes following Jen's fingers, Jack got the voice on that he usually saved for taking the mickey out of the kidlets: "Come on, Brigid. Even you have to admit — a twenty-year trip into the future is a pretty cool birthday present."

Brigid's head lifted slightly. "Oh, yes, it is. It is the present I left behind, however, that I'm afraid rather saddens me. My mother. My boyfriend...."

Jack winced, apparently realizing that his attempt at humor had hit a tree, and then his eyes widened. "Presents!" He leapt up. "I'll be right back!"

Brigid lifted her head to watch him scamper to the door and down the stairs, his semi-erection bobbing as he went. "He does have a nice penis, Jen."

"Indeed he does," she said, with a grin.

"It is very funny," said Brigid, "but I've never actually *seen* Tony's penis. I've touched it quite a lot, of course, which is lovely, but he was quite shy about letting me see it." She lifted her head and rested her chin on Jen's knee, gazing up.

Jen waited for a question, but none came. "Yes, Brigid. I've seen Tony's cock. Is that what you wanted to know?"

"Know?" Brigid tilted her head. "I want to know everything. I always have."

"Yeah."

Brigid hummed in agreement. Looking up, she rested her chin between Jen's knees. "You said just now that you had taken two trips out of your body. Did you mean orgasms?"

"Er, yes."

"Oh. Yes, I *think* I understand the reference. Did I actually give you an orgasm, then, when I touched your clitoris with my tongue?" There was nothing shy or suggestive about the question; Brigid looked at most mildly curious.

"Yes." Jen felt a small aftershock pass through her, and closed her eyes for a second.

"How interesting." Brigid's eyes floated downward in thought; Jen couldn't help feeling that those pale green eyes were drifting down to Jen's crotch. "I didn't think that that would happen. I'm very sorry, Jen."

"*Sorry?* Why on earth…?" *Out of darkness, infinite light.* Jen ran her fingers through her friend's flyaway hair. "You don't have to be sorry, Brigid, I promise."

Brigid frowned. "But orgasms are usually sexual." She blinked. "Aren't they?"

Having no idea where this was going, Jen could only chuckle. "Of course they are!"

Brigid's frown deepened into a kind of pout. A pout of perplexity. "I thought that a sexual act was supposed to involve a male and a female."

"Wh…?" Brigid didn't seem to be teasing; she was capable of joking, Jen remembered — or at least, thought she remembered — but seemed quite sincere. "Brigid. You… You do know that there are girls who have sex with other girls. And boys with boys. Right?"

"There are?" The pout dissipated as the eyes exploded to their full, astonishing width. "Truly?"

Laughing again, Jen shook her head. "Come on! You shared a dorm with Shirley for seven years! She was the president of the Gay and Lesbian Pride Club — it wasn't as if she were trying to hide the fact!"

Wide, wide, sea-green eyes blinked. "I… That was a group for people who were very happy and proud of their heritage, wasn't it? Didn't Shirley's family come from… Lesbos?"

"Scotland, I think," snorted Jen.

"Oh. She didn't look particularly Greek, it's true. I suppose it is unlikely that so many boys and girls would all have families from one Aegean island" Brigid's face seemed to contract, even as her eyes expanded once again. "Then... Shirley liked having sex with other girls?"

Jen goggled at her friend. "Why do you think Polly Philiaginedes and she shared a bed? You were the one who told *me* about that!"

"I..." Brigid seemed to be trying to calculate very quickly; her pupils shifted rapidly back and forth. "I thought they were trying to keep each other safe. Given all of the danger junior and senior year. They were quite good friends, you know."

"Not just friends, Bri."

"Oh."

"And... Not just sex, you know. Shirley and Polly have been married almost as long as me and Jack."

Brigid sat up, her face quite still. "They are married?"

"Yeah. Oh, crap — another thing you missed. Homosexual marriage has become legal in the territory since you... disappeared."

"Homosexual?"

It was almost impossible now for Jen to believe that her friend wasn't putting her on, but Brigid's face remained sincere and open, and Jen tried to answer in kind. "You know — gays, lesbians, people who love people who are the same gender? Homosexual? Same sex? Boys who love boys? Girls who — ?"

"OH!" In a moment, Brigid's expression shifted from confusion to the bright look of wonder that had been frozen on her face for twenty years. "I thought it meant people who like to have sex like everyone else — people who didn't like to deviate from the norm."

Again, Jen laughed. "The opposite, I think."

Cheeks pink, Brigid rested back against Jen's shins and looked down again. This time it was quite clear that she was indeed staring at Jen's crotch. "Jen? Did I have sex with *you*, just now, then?"

"I suppose." Jen felt herself pinkening too — felt her nipples tighten even as she was very aware of Brigid's poking against her legs. "Yeah."

"Does that mean that I've lost my virginity?"

"I don't..."

Brigid's face fell. "Oh. What a shame."

"I... I don't think it's... If you..."

"I do very much want to lose my virginity, you see." Over Brigid's head, Jen saw Jack enter the bedroom carrying a couple of packages. Brigid nodded, bouncing her head against Jen's knees. "And I don't foresee Tony being interested in having sex with me now. He is married."

Won't mean he won't want it, *thought Jen*, though I bet Maya wouldn't be exactly understanding. *She grimaced, and Jack frowned.*

Brigid cocked her head, so that her cheek was resting against Jen's left knee. "Am I wrong in that assumption as well? I'd always thought that married people don't have sex with other people, that that was one of the points of saying that you were married — but maybe that was just my parents."

As Jen tried to work out some response to that, she looked to Jack for help. He sat beside them, staring at the faded, wrapped packages in his hands — probably trying to avoid looking at Brigid. "No, of course not, of course you're right — at least, that isn't how it's supposed to work. But it does happen. Usually because one partner or the other can't keep... Can't stay faithful. And that's always bad. But sometimes... Like what's-her-name..." Now he looked to her for help.

Jen nodded. "Polly — we were just talking about them. She had a baby — two — with Shirley's brother Andrew because she and Shirley didn't want to use magical insemination."

"How interesting," said Brigid. "How did that work, do you think? Was Shirley there? I know that she and Andrew were quite close, but I wouldn't think that they'd have been interested in having sex together."

Jack look rather alarmed. "I... wouldn't think so."

"Hmm." Brigid slid down from Jen's knee and slithered up until her head was burrowed beneath Jen's chin, her arm wrapped beneath Jen's breast. "Is Tony fat now?"

Jack laughed.

"Well," Brigid continued, her breath tickling Jen's nipples, "you've both filled out rather nicely. Tony, however, was never quite active nor as fit as either of you. And so it seems to me that he might have got rather tubby over the past few years."

"The opposite, actually," said Jack, sounding as if he might be trying not to laugh. "He's..." Jack looked at Jen.

"He fell apart," she sighed. "When you... disappeared. He..." *He drank himself into oblivion. He nearly drove himself to an early grave before Maya straightened him out.* "He fell apart. And then, once he'd decided to... to move on, he became kind of a health nut."

Jen couldn't see Brigid's expression, but it felt as if she were frowning.

"He did lose a lot of his hair, though," Jen added, though she wasn't sure why.

"Oh," sighed Brigid, and she sounded somewhat happier. She wrapped herself even more tightly against Jen, curling her legs under Jen's ass.

Jack sat behind Brigid, his eyes fixed on the redhead's face. "He didn't paint at all for years."

"Oh." Now she didn't seem at all happy. "What a shame."

"Yeah," agreed Jack.

They lay there for a moment, and it felt oddly like the nights when Cynthia had wandered up to their bed after a nightmare and snuggled herself between them, trying desperately to get back to sleep. Though at the moment, the feelings running through Jen didn't seem to be tending toward the motherly. She looked over to her husband. The look on his face was like nothing that she had ever seen there before. Stoic, definitely — a perennial expression of his. Concerned. Horny.

Definitely not fatherly.

She winked at him, and he startled out of whatever revery she'd lost him to.

"Presents," he said, his voice thick as if he hadn't used it for weeks.

"Presents?" asked Brigid, turning her head toward him while keeping her body glued to Jen's.

He held up two packages, wrapped in the same midnight blue paper. The memory flooded back to Jen: wrapping these together the morning of Brigid's party. They'd had a fight over — what? Jack's present? And then they'd had a really great make-up fuck. A *flying* fuck....

And then going up to this house with all of the drunk partygoers. Finding the... *thing* out in the yard. Finding Mrs. O'Danan's body. And finding nothing else.

He was staring down at the presents. "I brought these here when we couldn't find you. Figured... You should have them, whenever..." He looked up, and a new set of emotions seemed to be adding themselves to the ones that had already been there: sorrow, pain, joy.

Tears began to squeeze Jen's eyes even as the thought flooded through her: he too had hoped for Brigid's return. It hadn't just been her.

He shrugged. "They've been in your night stand all of this time. Thought you might like to open them." Brigid disengaged herself from

Jen, and they both turned toward him. He placed the presents on the bed. "The big one's Jen's."

"Well," Brigid said, very seriously, "I can't decide which one to save for last."

"Open hers first," said Jack, shooting Jen a shy, sly grin.

At first she thought he must be up to something, but then she remembered her gift, and realized that his discomfort hadn't dissipated entirely. She pulled the larger package in front of Brigid. "Go on."

Pulling her wand from her hair, Brigid daintily began to dispel the Spell-o-tape that held the package together. Jen had forgot this: Brigid hated to tear any of the paper. One after another, she pealed away the layers of gauzy wrapping revealing at last the distinctive maroon and lavender box from Francesca's, the territory's only dress shop for decades. Jen hadn't seen one in years, since Frances Ball had retired, breaking Emi Kamiyama's heart.

Jen suddenly felt as if the box shouldn't be opened — this was almost certainly the last unopened present from her mother's favorite store.

Fortunately, she was able to hold the impulse in; Brigid opened the box and lifted out the filmy length of silk that was nestled within. "Ooo!" She held it up.

Jack's face dropped. Clearly, like Jen, he hadn't remembered her gift being quite so... little. Sheer. Flimsy.

Brigid started waving it, as if she were trying it out as a signal flag. Watching the emerald green fabric flutter.

Jen cleared her throat. "It's a nightie."

"Oh." Brigid smiled brightly, even as her brows bunched, so that she looked — for her — rather dubious. "I thought maybe it was a rather lovely scarf."

"It's charmed... I'll show you." Jen held out her hand and Brigid let the long, narrow swath of silk flow into her fingers. "Stand up."

Dutifully, Jen's friend slid over Jack's legs and off the side of the bed. Jen's husband pulled his knees to his chest to let Jen by — probably also to hide his own reaction. Poor boy. As Jen rolled past him to sit on the edge of the bed, she let the silk of the nightie trail across his shins. Just so he shouldn't feel *too* comfortable sitting on a bed with two naked women. He grimaced and pulled his knees tight.

Jen snorted and turned to her friend, who was standing as she'd been told. Running the fabric behind Brigid's ass, she murmured, "Lift."

"Lift?"

"Your hands."

Again, Brigid obeyed.

As Jen wrapped the silk over Brigid's hips, she thought, *How ridiculous. What was I thinking getting her this?* And then she thought, *I never felt ridiculous wearing mine.* Carefully, she crossed the nightie at Brigid's crotch and then held the ends up in front of Brigid's breasts. "Hold," she ordered.

Obedient still, Brigid to the ends of the gauzy fabric.

"Against your, er, yabos."

"Oh."

Jen realized that the yabos in question — the gorgeous yabos in question — were right at her eye level. That she felt like falling into the gorge between them. That Jack had dreamed, had beat off at the idea of squeezing himself there... Jen shivered, and reached back to pick up Jack's wand. Carefully she tapped it against each breast, and then over Brigid's pubes.

The silk suddenly clung to Brigid's flesh like paint.

Brigid gave a breathy "Oh!" Taking her hands away, she looked down with delight. "How lovely!" She wiggled a bit to see if the charm would hold, and of course it did — these *lovely*, naughty things were designed to stay in place through a hell of a lot more than a little shimmy — but Jen found herself mesmerized by the undulation. By the way that she could have counted the bumps on Brigid's nipples through the silk. If she'd wanted.

Brigid turned and wiggled again, looking over her own shoulder at her ass, at the way that the draped silk shook, even as Jen took in the way that the green accentuated the impossible whiteness of Brigid's skin, that the scoop of the silk across that lovely butt accentuated the length of that straight, supple back. Brigid turned back, still moving, and the charm at her crotch held perfectly, so that Jen couldn't actually see Brigid's privates, but the concealment only made her more aware of what was hidden.

(More naked than naked.)

Jen heard Jack take a sharp breath behind her.

"Oh," gasped Brigid, running her hands over the silk. "Thank you! It's quite lovely!" She leaned down, and Jen's whole world was suddenly all the glow of emerald eyes and the light, quick press of surprisingly full lips against Jen's own. "What a nice present! It is charmed for warmth, I see, which is pleasant. It can get quite chilly here at night. Is it for having sex in?"

"Yes," answered Jack tersely.

"Oh," sighed Brigid again, though this time wistfully. "How nice."

"I figured," said Jen, "that Tony wouldn't be able to keep his hands off you after he saw you in that."

Jack grunted.

"Oh. Thank you. He had said that we could fuck, you know. Tonight. That night. My birthday. Though I suppose you didn't know. I didn't get a chance to talk to you about it and I don't suppose Tony would have spoken to either of you —"

"No," Jack said.

"Hmm."

Jen tore her eyes away from the impossible way that her gift fit and followed her friend's body and picked up the other, smaller package. "Jack's gift next."

Smiling widely, Brigid took the present and repeated the painstaking process of removing the wrapping.

Jen looked over at her husband again, still curled in on himself against the headboard, and gave him a smirk. He favored her with a grim, fleeting smile.

"Ooo." Brigid lifted another length of green silk from a small, velvet bag. Charmed to it was a small, simple, silver broach bearing a small emerald that Jen could see matched the glow of Brigid's eyes perfectly. As Jack had said it would. Brigid held the jewel up. "This is beautiful."

"We had a hell of a fight about that, the day you disappeared."

"A fight?"

"It's a choker," Jack said. "Here, let me have my wand." When Jen handed it back to him, he moved closer, still managing somehow to keep his knees up in front of what Jen suspected was a full-blown boner. "Now put the choker around your neck, Brigid."

She did and Jack tapped the silk, sealing the charm. Wriggling once again in excitement, Brigid skipped over to the vanity and examined the jewel at her throat in the mirror.

Jack slid up behind Jen, and she could feel that, yes, he was indeed hard again. He said, "We had a fight because Jen thought that it was a bit... excessive."

"Hmm?" Brigid blinked back at them.

"I guess she thought you'd be embarrassed. Or Tony might be, because he couldn't."

"Oh."

"Yeah, that," Jen said, remembering that those were exactly the reasons she'd spelled out to him that morning when he'd sprung the idea on her. "But mostly... I think I was jealous."

"Jealous?" Brigid's eyes widened alarmingly, flashing in the candlelight along with the jewel at her throat. "Oh, if you want it for yourself, I —"

"No," said Jen. "It's meant to be yours. Jealous, not because you got that jewel, because he's given me many over the years" — emeralds, diamonds, children, memories — "but... It seemed like something you'd give someone you really liked. Not just a friend."

Brigid sat back down on the bed, frowning, and touched Jen's foot. "Oh, but Jen, you know that Jack wouldn't ever fancy me, he has only ever felt friendship toward me. And I am quite pleased with that!" Smiling, she touched Jack's bare knee with her other hand.

"Er," choked Jack.

Jen laid her hand atop Brigid's. "As a matter of fact, Bri, that's not exactly true."

"I sure that you never had cause to be jealous of me." Brigid frowned.

"Maybe not," granted Jen. "But Jack..."

Her husband's arms tightened around Jen's waist. "I did, uh, *fancy* you, Brigid. A lot."

"No, I am certain that you did not."

"I did. I swear. I may not even have known that that was what it was, but —"

"No," Brigid said, and stood. "You see, no one fancies me. I'm odd, and my eyes make people uncomfortable." She crossed her arms in front of her barely-clad breasts and looked toward the door.

"You're wrong," said Jack, the bullheaded, sweet idiot. "Tony fancied you a hell of a lot. And Gabe fancied you, even if he never managed to say anything about it. Hell, Rhea was looking at you today like you were breakfast, lunch *and* dessert." He laughed, but Brigid looked at him blankly. "Brigid. I was attracted to you. I had a crush on. I did. Don't... You're a beautiful young woman. I — That's the reason that I wanted to give you the jewel. It was just sitting in my safety deposit box, it was some old relative's apparently, and when I found it, you can see it sort of glows, and I immediately thought, Brigid glows like that, and I knew I had to give it to you. So that everyone — Tony, everyone — would see how beautiful you are."

"Oh," said Brigid tonelessly. "Thank you both so very much for the lovely presents." She turned as if to walk back to the door.

Jen took her wrist and stopped her. "Don't, Brigid. It's true."

"No, I am afraid that it is not. I am capable of looking in the mirror. I know what I see there, and it is nothing like what I see in front of me. And while I do not always understand why people think the rather unexpected things that they do, I do watch how they behave. I do not know about Rhea, I suppose, but Gabe never acted toward me as if he found me at all sexually attractive, nor, Jack, did you. Nor did Tony, which rather hurt."

"Brigid," whispered Jen, "he did, he —"

"Men who fancy women generally do not do everything that they can to avoid fucking those women."

"Brigid, sweetheart," Jen said, "it's the opposite. He cared for you too much. I... He wanted it to be perfect for you."

Brigid smiled sadly and shook her head, the emerald at her throat winking in the candlelight. "I am afraid that I cannot subscribe to that theory. Maybe if I had got him to fuck me to... *that* night, then I might feel differently. However, he did not. Look at his relationship with you, Jen. He certainly fancied you, yet that did not stop him from accepting your virginity."

The long-forgotten, disappointing ridiculousness of that whole mess flooded back for the first time in decades. "Yeah, well, look how well that turned out."

"Nonetheless, he was interested in you in a way that he was clearly never interested in me."

Jen could feel Jack all but growl in frustration against her back. "Come on, Brigid. You want behavior? If I didn't think you were attractive, then why have I been hiding my erection against my wife's ass since you put that ridiculous part of filth on?"

Brigid's mouth and eyes opened wide. "Filth?"

"That... silk... thing."

"Oh." Brigid looked down. The ends of the charmed silk barely covered the tops of her areolae. Between the two emerald strips, her pale skin was slowly turning pink. She gazed back up, hugely. "You have an erection, Jack?"

He tried to laugh, but to Jen's ear it was a pathetic attempt.

It was at that point that Jen realized where all of this was headed.

Where they were going. Where *she* wanted it… Her tips — finger, nose, nipples, all — buzzed as if with cold, but she did not feel cold at all. Still, she was frozen.

Brigid sat back down, her sorrow apparently forgotten. "May I see it?"

"Brigid…" Jack groaned, but the name acted on Jen as it had that whole day, warming her, prompting her. She slid from between Jack's legs: she could feel a strand of precum pull taut between her lower back and the tip of Jack's cock. Could feel it *snap.*

"Oh," said Brigid's, staring at the hard-on between Jen's husband's legs with fascination. "I have never seen an erection before. It looks very nice."

"Thanks!" As Jack laughed again rather manically, Jen slid beside her friend and peered back at the very familiar cock that stood there, at the ready. "You've never…?"

"No. Hmm," said Brigid, and then turned to Jen. "May I… touch it?"

Jack snorted another, somewhat more successful laugh. "How come you're asking her?"

"Oh." Brigid's eyes narrowed, but had focussed back on the cock under consideration. "The penis is yours, after all. I suppose that I was thinking that the erection is hers."

This time it was Jen who laughed, nerves sparkling. "No, Bri. That's the point he was trying to make. That's all yours." Long, long ago, Jen's dad had explained how mundane car motors were driven by hundreds of tiny explosions per second, so that they only sounded like a smooth growl. Her heart felt… "Can she, Jack? Touch?" He gawked at her. "Please?"

He stared down idiotically, as if maybe he'd thought they had been talking about something other than his dark red, emphatic hard-on. "Jen… I don't…." He gave a whimpering sigh. Really, it had had two good workouts already today. It should be happily asleep, as they all should, if they didn't have other things on their minds. Clearly he wanted this. He turned his face away from them, but nodded.

Swift as snakestrike, long, white fingers wrapped themselves around a length of flesh that Jen knew that no one but she had ever touched before. Jack gasped and looked up, his eyes locking with hers. The whites showed, panicked.

Brigid hummed, running her fingertips up his length.

"Brigid." Jen touched her friend's naked back. "Do you want to know why I was screaming your name just now?"

Nodding, Brigid continued to explore Jack's erection. Jen had only ever seen her like this when she was examining one of Schuler's crazier, rarer creatures.

"Jack," Jen said, watching anxiety and pleasure war in her husband's face, "do you want to tell her?"

He let out a groan, closed his eyes, but began to speak. "My senior year. Your junior... Jen was seeing Tony. And you went with me..."

He gasped as Brigid's index finger explored his cock head, drawing patterns on the dark skin with the stream of clear fluid that was pooling at the tip. Leaning forward, licking her lips unselfconsciousy, Brigid finished the phrase for him. "...as friends to the Christmas Dance. It was lovely."

Jack groaned again. "You... That night. I'd been... whacking off like crazy, months, thinking about..."

Brigid reached out with her other hand, and Jack's jaw dropped open.

"About me," said Jen.

"Of course he did." Brigid's left hand weighed his balls. "I..." She fell uncharacteristically silent.

Jen needed them to say what they weren't saying. Needed this to happen soon before she lost her courage. "You went home that night, jumped into your bed, still in that silver dress, and diddled yourself for hours until you fell asleep, imagining it was Jack touching you."

For one of the first time that Jen could remember, Brigid began to turn pink not from excitement but — apparently — embarrassment. "Yes." Her hands remained frozen on Jack's cock. "I did. And for many nights after that."

Jen slid up behind Brigid. "Yeah. You told me. But that night, Jack was in his own bed, that nice, thick cock in his own hands, stroking himself just like you're doing."

"Thinking about you."

Jen's finger's trembled, but found their way to the bare sides of Brigid's breasts, and Brigid gave a whimper, her grip of Jack tightening slightly.

"AH!" gasped Jack, but then he gritted his teeth and stared at Brigid — at both of them. "No. *Shit*. No... You. Brigid. Thought about... Thought about you. Thought about you. About..."

"About your tits." Jen run her fingers across the front of those very breasts — breasts she had touched as stone, but that were now soft, and warm and silk-clad. "About touching them. About pushing his cock between them." Brigid whimpered again, and whimpered again as Jen pinched thickening nipples. "Beat off for months after, thinking about you. About you."

"No."

Jack hissed, "Yes. I told her. Before we found... Found you. This afternoon. And she..."

"I pretended. To be you. Fucking him."

Jack reached out, his hands joining Jen's. "Before... and after, this... Just now, again, I did, fucked her tits, her pretending, and then I.... We pretended you were going down on her. Because we both think... think... You're beautiful, Brigid."

Whispering into Brigid's ear, her lips touching the lobe, her breath fanning Brigid's hair in a way that Jen knew drove Jack wild, she said, "We both got off, pretending to get to make love to you. To you." She let her fingers trail down from beneath Jack's, following the silk path downward, across the bellies of her breasts, along her ribs, to either side of her navel...

Brigid shuddered, and her hand flew from Jack's balls, stopping Jen's progress.

They all froze.

And Brigid suddenly seemed to be freezing, in spite of Francesca's warming charms: her teeth chittered and her stomach trembled. "J-j-j..."

They waited.

Brigid turned her face away from Jen's. Very, very quietly, through still-quivering jaws, she said. "I have... a p-p-present... that I should like to g-give you... if you...." The shivering overtook her.

Jen embraced her from behind, and Jack wrapped his thin, strong arms around them both. Brigid's hand was still on his rod, but his voice dropped back down into a coital, cunt-quickening register. "Whatever you want to give us, Brigid, we'd be honored to have."

Brigid gave what felt and sounded like a sob, but quickly took a deep breath that squeezed them all closer together. "I... May I give you m-my... my virginity?" Another spasm of shivering. "P-please?"

"We would love that," Jack said, and leaned his face forward. Jen thought he was going to kiss Brigid — felt a wild twang of jealousy and horniness zip through her — but his lips found hers, and their heat banished all fear, all cold. He backed off again, his eyes on hers.

Jen nodded, and Jack brushed those fabulous thin lips of his against

Brigid's softer, fuller ones.

Brigid stopped breathing — it felt as if her heart had stopped as well — until Jen whispered into her ear, "We would love to. It would be our pleasure."

Brigid moaned.

8 — Equilateral

Jack and Brigid kissed on, and Jen felt another ridiculous shiver of jealousy flutter up inside of her.

Jealous? Why? This was her idea — or at least, partially hers. She nibbled on Brigid's ear, and let her hand trail down to where Brigid's fingers were still loosely curled around Jack's cock. Looking her childish churlishness in the face, she wrapped her fingers around Brigid's so that they were tight against Jack's flesh, and moved her friend's hand down and then up again.

They both groaned, mouths muffling mingled delight.

Jen smiled. Giving Brigid's ear a good, long lick, she whispered, "He likes it when you squeeze like that. He's come twice already tonight — and he's not a nineteen-year-old any more. No need to be timid."

Following Jen's advice, Brigid gave a long pull on his shaft, and then let loose a high-pitched sigh into Jack's mouth; he answered it with a low groan.

"The part from the head to the middle is the most sensitive. He likes that a lot."

"Hmm," answered Brigid in Jack's mouth, and followed Jen's directions.

Feeling a bit more centered — if no more in control — Jen let go of Brigid's hand, which continued to stroke Jen's husband steadily. Jen's fingertips found soft flesh — Brigid's inner thigh, she realized: smooth, soft. Fingers traveled at their own direction, five wanderers meandering towards a common goal with no sense of urgency. They reached a curtain of silk — Francesca's finest — and, slipping beneath it, they found a thatch of hair, and Brigid jumped, causing Jack to groan again.

Brigid's pubic curls were finer than Jack's — finer, even, than Jen's own. "When we used to lie on your bed, nattering on about boys and penises and fucking," Jen whispered, "did you ever think of reaching over and touching me?"

Brigid shook her head, gasping as Jack nipped lightly at her throat.

"Me neither," Jen admitted, and found that she was truly sad to say this. "Why didn't we? There we both were, horny as hell — why didn't we help each other out?" She let her fingers slide down through that fine copse of hair to the warm, moist flesh below — labia open, as they had been during Brigid's long incarceration. Jen's index and middle fingers slid along the lengths of those wet, tight lips, and Brigid threw her head back onto Jen's shoulder.

"D-didn't kn-know girls could…"

Jack took advantage of the opening to nibble around the underside of Brigid's chin.

Brigid arched, whimpering.

"I knew," sighed Jen, licking her way down Brigid's jugular as her husband ran his teeth along Brigid's Adam's apple — both of them pulling at the choker as they passed it.. She leaned forward and they kissed, there beneath Brigid's chin, tongues dancing, as Jen's fingers stroked unselfconsciously up and down along the fine, slick ridges of the flesh that spread beneath them.

It was her favorite way of playing with herself — had been since she first tried it. No doubt it's what she was doing while she slept, if she was to believe Jack and Brigid. Was it Bri's? As Jack moved on, kissing his way down to Brigid's high clavicles, Jen tried to remember. She hadn't really felt comfortable *looking* at Brigid while each of them played with herself. Circles, maybe? Jen experimented, letting first one fingertip and then two swirl around the diamond-hard bump at the front.

Brigid shuddered, a high sigh floating down into a low moan.

"That feel good?" Jen asked, knowing the answer.

"Oh… yes. Yes, it feels quite nice."

Quite nice. Bri. Even with Jack licking at the slope above her breasts and Jen playing tarantellas on her clit, she was still Bri. It was wonderful. "Good."

"Extremely nice. I —" Brigid began, but interrupted herself with another healthy groan. Jack had clamped on to one of Brigid's nipples through the silk; he was probably tweaking the other, though Jen couldn't see. The gooseflesh that erupted along Brigid's throat tickled Jen's cheek, her lips.

"Told you he loved your breasts."

"Y-yes." Brigid arched again as Jack switched nipples, and then went limp, beginning to slide off of Jen's shoulder.

Continuing to stroke her friend, Jen used the free arm to cradle Brigid, until she was almost lying down across Jen's lap. *Supine...*

Jack began to kiss and lick his way down the bare trail between the two swaths of silk that trailed down Brigid's white belly, and Brigid pushed her tummy up, arching again and turning so that her face rolled toward Jen and mouth opened. As if it were the most natural thing in the world, her lips latched on to Jen's nipple, sending sparks of flame shooting from that spot to Jen's clit and out to every extremity.

God, thought Jen, *Oh, God, she's...*

Brigid's mouth pulled at Jen's breast as if she were indeed seeking nourishment, and Jen looked down to find huge, pale green eyes open and staring up at her.

Then Jack kissed his way around Jen's hand. That amazing mouth found Brigid's lips and then began to dance with Jen's fingers, and Brigid gasped, her mouth loosening itself from Jen. Brigid fell back across Jen's legs, transported.

Brigid's eyes, though, remained focused on Jen's — well, maybe not focused, but were they ever?

Pulling her legs out, Jen leaned down. Copper-colored eyebrows arched impossibly high until they disappeared from sight and Jen's mouth caressed Brigid's.

Such a different mouth — so much softer than Jack's, and warm. Sweet taste. *Sweet.*

Jen's breasts slid up along Brigid's, and somehow that, the bump of her nipples against Brigid's, the slide of soft flesh against her flesh, was the feeling that set her off — that told her what she was doing. She was making love to another woman. (*Fucking? Is this...?*) Making love to Brigid.

Brigid gasped into Jen's mouth. The puff of air across her tongue, and the hum of it sent a shiver through Jen.

She and Jack were making love to Brigid.

Brigid, who even Jen had been ready to give up as dead not six hours before.

She was making love to Brigid and it felt....

Wonderful.

Jen pushed up and gazed down: Brigid's eyes were even more

unfocused than usual. There were bite marks and a small, cupid's-bow bruise on the ivory flesh of the neck where Jen and Jack had nibbled.

Jen felt Jack's mouth working around her fingers. Felt Brigid's clit stiffening and quivering. Watched as Brigid's huge eyes flickered, opened wide, and crossed.

"I think, Bri," she said, "I think I want to taste you too."

"Hmm."

"Want me to?"

"Hmmm." It sounded like an assent to Jen.

With another shiver and a grin, she leaned down and kissed a silk-clad nipple, glorying as it rose between her lips.

Jen had fantasized about sleeping with other people. Everyone did. And if she thought about it, she'd even had a fantasy or two about being in a group — men and women, caressing her, fucking her.

When she'd flown competitively, everyone assumed that all of the women were queer, but really there'd only been a few. And none of them had ever come on to her. But once or twice, after a race on the road somewhere — in Hexenhavn or Puerto de las Brujas — they'd all gone out dancing, and who else was there to dance with? She wasn't going to dance with the fans — they all learned to keep that line very clear or end up kicked off the circuit.

And dancing with Melissa Somes, say, who had amazing eyes and could move on the dance floor as Jen had always wished she could — as Jack, wonderful as he was, could never even attempt... There would come a moment when Melissa would open those eyes — dark brown in a way that was totally unlike Jack's — and they would both stand there, on a knife edge, before they'd both start giggling and whirling around the floor like a pair of nine-year-olds.

Had Jen ever really thought of stepping over that line? Melissa, who during Jen's time on the team slept with three or four of the other racers, a couple of whom Jen had been sure were, if anything, straighter than she was. Melissa, who was always flying over before a race and pointiing out the the biggest pair of yabos in the crowd. Or Arathusa, with her long, mahogany fingers...?

Not really. No. Any more than she'd considered reaching over when she was lying next to a naked Brigid, as they rubbed themselves sore, groaning and giggling and sighing.

But the flesh beneath her lips now was flesh she hungered to taste.

The groans of pleasure buzzing up from the belly beneath her tongue pleasured Jen. She felt alive. She felt awake and wonderful raw as she hadn't felt...

Jen withdrew her hand from Brigid's clit and Brigid's groan now was one of disappointment. Trailing a most finger over a silk-covered hip, she looked down at her husband, happily lapping away at Brigid's pussy. Jen loved watching him do this — no surprise, since before now, she'd always been the one he was lapping at. But now she found that the sight itself was erotic: Jack nose bobbing, his eyes half-lidded. "Share?" she asked, the sound of the words low, so that she felt her chest rumbling against Brigid's belly.

Those lids flew open, the eyes beneath flashing brightly. His nose bobbed more as he nodded.

Determined not to think about what she was doing — determined simply to do it — Jen leaned forward. *Kissing Jack*, she thought. *I'm going to kiss...*

Only Jack had never grown a beard — couldn't, really — and so the fine, copper curls of Brigid's bush kept Jen from pretending.

Her nose brushed against Jack's, and a rich, tart scent filled the nostrils, *scintillating*. A scent she had only ever smelled before at a distance, or on Jack's face, or on his cock, eating him after they'd already fucked — not something they'd done much lately, but this evening, her cuntscent had been there faintly when she tasted him, and now —

And now, she reached out with her tongue, and intertwined it with his, two tongues dancing around Brigid's clit like eels mating around a particularly soft, sensitive rock. The taste was different — lighter than her own, and almost sweet, like Brigid's mouth.

"*Jennifer!*" Brigid lowed, as if the pleasure were too much; she twisted, grabbing on to Jen's calf, and Jen wasn't sure whether her friend was trying to pull her close or buck her off.

But the weight of Jen's chest and the promise of two tongues on Brigid's cunt held her pelvis still, even as her head and arms turned and pulled.

Brigid pulled Jen's leg close, Jen's toes cramming themselves into Brigid's mouth, and Brigid let out a long, muffled scream.

Jack's right hand snaked up along Brigid's long belly, first brushing Jen's nipple and then trekking up onto Brigid's, where Jen knew he would clamp down, gentle but firm, in counterpoint to his tongue's ministrations. Usually he would use both, but…

But Jen was here, swapping the taste of Brigid's excitement with him. No reason for her to go without though. Jen's left hand, which had been resting on Brigid's fluttering tummy slid up to play with the other breast — so that it shouldn't feel lonely.

She found her other hand, which had been cupped beneath Brigid's ass, sliding up beneath Jack's chin, the index finger extended. Jack's tongue broke from the duet that they were performing long enough to wet the finger thoroughly before flicking back up against her own, and then the finger found the opening to Brigid's cunt and slid in.

Brigid's body became absolutely still, and for a moment Jen was terrified that she'd hurt her friend, But then Jen felt the hot, slick walls of Brigid's cunt clench around her finger and begin to spasm, and Brigid bellowed so loudly that, even with a mouth full of Jen's foot, it seemed as if the sound would bring the old house around them crashing down to the ground.

• •

"Are you okay, Brigid?" Jack's fingers flew up to her pale, still throat, just below the emerald choker.

Jen stared down at Brigid's face, which was as drained of color as it had been when they had found her, but slack, her enormous eyes rolled back in her head. "*Brigid?*" Jen began to reach for her wand, but Jack already had it, and had begun the wand movement for a *Trezeste*.

"I see what you meant about leaving your body," said Brigid — somehow without moving a muscle. "That was very interesting."

Jen found that she had been holding her breath. In Brigid-speak, apparently, *very interesting* could mean either *absolutely fucking fantastic* or *a near-death experience.*

Jack brushed the hair out of Brigid's face. "You okay?"

"Oh, yes," said Brigid, eyes floating back more or less to the front of her head. "I'm doing quite nicely. I've never had someone else excite me to orgasm, so I suppose it caught me unprepared."

"Just a bit," snorted Jen.

Jack chuckled, but his expression remained grave. "That… was probably a bit much. We probably shouldn't —"

"Oh, please fuck me, Jack." Brigid reached out and grabbed Jack's cock — grabbed it with authority, as Jen had encouraged her to do earlier, which left Jack looking as if he'd been hit in the stomach with a bludger. "I can't imagine whether fucking might be any more stimulating, but I am fairly certain that the sensation won't do any lasting damage," she sighed, and then cocked her head. "Though I am willing to chance it."

Jen giggled. They both looked at her — Brigid's gaze open, Jack's astonished. She leaned forward to kiss each of them. Funny: she wasn't even going to be participating in the main event, and yet her heart was beating wildly in her throat. "So, how do you two want to do this?"

Now Brigid was the one who blinked. "Do?" She looked up at Jack.

He gave them his pained smile. "I... I don't know, Brigid. I mean, it's not like I've done this before." When Brigid's eyes widened astonishingly, he spluttered, "I mean, with someone who was, you know, like you. A virgin."

"Oh." The huge green eyes swiveled from Jack to Jen and back again. "Oh."

"In fact," he said, staring down at her hand on his prick, "I... I've never done this with anyone but Jen."

"Oh." Brigid's long fingers released Jack, who let out a huff of either relief or disappointment. Maybe both. Those long fingers reached up to stroke Jen's cheek, though her gaze stayed on Jen's husband. "Oh."

"I want to, to do this," Jack said, still looking down. "I just don't know..."

"No," agreed Brigid. Jen wasn't sure what she was agreeing with. Now Brigid looked up at Jen. "I want to do this too, rather a lot. I want to fuck Jack, very much. Only, it doesn't seem right for *him* to fuck *me*, does it?"

After a moment of Brigid looking thoughtfully sad and Jack looking stoic, Jen couldn't take it — of *course*, once again, she was the one to see the way through. "No problem." Leaning forward, she slid onto Brigid's body, the moment when her breasts bobbled against Brigid's silk-encased ones once again sending a spark to her clit. She kissed Brigid, who lay back, wide-eyed, as Jen threw a leg across Brigid's waist. Looking back at Jack, she whispered, "Like to fuck me this way, don't you, Jack?" She lifted her bottom up and wiggled it at him, like a matador waving a cape before a bull.

Jack's face darkened and his mouth dropped open.

In point of fact, taking her on her hands and knees was his favorite way to fuck — not that he didn't seem to like them all. She preferred to face him, but mostly because she'd found over the years that the front of her cunt was more sensitive than the back; if his cock where curved in the other direction, like Tony's…

Jen reached down between her legs — but instead of readying her own privates for Jack's arrival, she lifted the nightie and stroked Brigid's. Brigid stared up at her with an expression of absolute sensual abandon.

"Jen," Jack groaned. "Brigid…"

"C'mon, baby," sighed Jen, still looking down into Brigid's misty gaze. "Fuck me."

Jack's hands skimmed lightly over Jen's ass. "Are… Are you on the Charm?"

"Uh-huh," sighed Jen and Brigid in harmony.

"I…"

"No one's ever fucked my cunt, Jack," Jen moaned. "Fuck me." Jen's thumb circled Brigid's clit as one finger dipped back in to her tight hole.

"*Shit!*" When Jack began swearing, it was always a good sign. He slide up behind her, and Jen felt Brigid's legs spread, welcoming him.

"Baby," Jen found herself saying — not knowing which of them she was talking to, realizing that it was to both of them. "It might… hurt a bit at first. Take your time, okay? Go slow. Breathe."

"Always," groaned Jack, "always wanted to be… your first."

"Mmm," agreed Brigid, her groan becoming throatier as Jen slid her finger further in.

Jack's cock slid along Jen's wrist, insinuating itself up against Jen's own entrance, and for a moment, she almost gave in and pushed back, spearing herself on him. But she had had that opportunity often — once earlier that day. This was not her turn. She slid her finger out of Brigid and grasped Jack's rod by the root. "Breathe," she said.

Brigid was quivering — with anticipation, but also with fear, probably.

"Breathe," Jen repeated, and slid the tip of Jack's cock along Brigid's slit, picking up some lubrication, but also giving the clit a nice introduction to its new playmate.

Brigid let out a long, breathy sigh, and then gulped in a huge lungful as Jen positioned the head of Jack's cock against Brigid's cunt; her eyes squeezed shut.

"Wait," said Jack, his fingers digging into Jen's haunches. He leaned forward, so that Brigid's raised thighs pressed, trembling, against Jen's ass and lower back. "Wait."

He grabbed Jen's wand, which lay on the bed, and began mumbling what Jen thought was a conjuration. Brigid's face began to glow even more warmly; green eyes flickered back open. *"Ooo!"*

Jen looked up. Jack had conjured a circle of candles, levitated around them, bathing the bed and the bodies in it in a golden, tremulous light. *A circle of flame, to protect and contain...* He leaned forward and kissed the back of Jen's neck, even while reaching down with his wand hand and caressing Brigid's cheek. "I... want it to be the way you dreamed."

Brigid's face expanded; Jen had only seen that expression on her friend's face once before: when Jen had brought her out to the Grey Forest during their first week at the Mountain and showed her that unicorns weren't mythical creatures after all.

"We don't have a bronze thingamee," Jen murmured.

Brigid leaned up and whispered in Jen's ear, "You will by my calyx." Then she deposited a gentle kiss in Jen's ear, leaned back, and closed her eyes again. Where it had been a grimace a moment before, however, now it was an expression of peace.

"Ready?" Jen asked.

"Yes," the other two said.

Jen reached back between her legs again, past her own pubes and the silk curtain covering Brigid's. She grasped Jack's cock and brought it back to Brigid's cunt. "Take in a deep breath," she said, "and let it out."

As they both exhaled, Jen pulled Jack forward against the thin barrier guarding the entrance to Brigid's cunt; Brigid began to tense again, and so — without considering — Jen leaned down and sucked one of Brigid's glorious, tight, nightie-covered nipples *hard*.

Brigid cried out, and Jack pressed against Jen's back. Brigid gasped again, lifting her pelvis, trapping Jen's hand between it and Jen's own.

Jen could feel three textures of pubic hair tickling her fingers. Could feel moisture. Brigid let out a low, quick grunt, and Jen added her teeth, gently...

Around her, Jack and Brigid both shuddered.

Letting the nipple slip from between her lips, feeling the two hearts hammering against her cheek and her back, she whispered, "Shh... Shh..."

"Oh," said Brigid, her voice high and wispy. "Oh."

"So... *tight*," Jack hissed.

Hasn't given birth to your three little monsters, has she? thought Jen, but she said, "Feels nice." It did, too: squeezed between the two of them…

"Mmm," agreed her lovers, the hum of their voices warming Jen front and back.

Brigid pushed up again. "F-fuck…"

Jack obliged, burying himself more deeply, and Brigid let out a pant that sounded at first like a moan of pain, but turned into a giggle. "*Oh… OHhhee!*"

Jen felt Jack's chest buck against her chest, felt a puff of surprised laughter against her neck, and chuckled herself. "Okay?"

"Oh, yes, yes… *Ohhee!* Hurts a… a bit, but… feels quite… *nice.*"

"Good," said Jen with a smile. "Nice is… good."

Air cooled the small of Jen's back as Jack withdrew slightly, and gooseflesh erupted all over Brigid's chest, belly, the fronts of her thighs, tickling Jen's skin. Taking a deep breath, Jen looked down at Brigid. "Think it's okay to go a little harder?"

Brigid blinked and part her lip, but then smiled and nodded.

Leaning forward again, Jen kissed Brigid; the sweet, full taste was growing more familiar, but the sensation still sizzled through Jen's veins. "Fuck me. No need to be timid."

Jack growled, and his mouth latched onto the back of her neck. Brigid hissed and moaned as that lovely penis she'd been admiring began to plunge and withdraw.

For some time, Jen lay there between them, excited by their grunts of excitement, by the whisper of their flesh against hers, excited, even, by Brigid's occasional giggles. She tried to begin to play with Brigid's clit with the fingers that were still trapped between — (*among?*) — their pelvises, but Brigid winced. Clearly too much. And so Jen withdrew the hand and settled for kissing her friend and enjoying the feeling of Jack's thrusts bouncing their jubblies together. She hadn't thought about breasts much before — not having much of her own to think about.

But now she thought maybe she saw boys' fascinations with them a bit more clearly. They looked nice, and they definitely said *I'm a girl! Yoohoo!* But they felt… amazing. And Brigid's lips…

Then Jack's hand snaked down between their bellies, and Jen was about to tell him not to, that Brigid didn't want —

But his fingers found *her* clit, and suddenly, instead of being an observer, the medium through which they were fucking, she found herself a participant, and *OOO…*

She arched up against her husband — how often had they fucked this way? — and his kisses on her neck grew harder, until they were nibbles, and then bites.

"Fuck, fuck, Jen," he groaned.

"Fuck me, fuck me, fuck me," she gasped, forgetting that, in fact, hers wasn't the cunt he was plowing. Forgetting. Not caring.

She lost herself in the flow of flesh beneath and against her, and was shocked when a hungry mouth latched itself onto one of her dangling, bouncing nipples. "Shit!"

Brigid tittered again against Jen's breast, sucking hard. *No need to be timid.*

Jack's free hand managed to flick Jen's other nipple before departing; Jen was about to complain when she heard and felt a gasp against her other breast. Jack had clearly moved to Brigid's nipple, the good boy. He muttered into Jen's ear, his voice rising, "Shit. Shit. *Shit.*"

Brigid suddenly dropped back, quivering, her eyes rolling back into her head once more.

"SHIT. *SHIT!*"

Then Brigid began to laugh — not the fluttery giggle from before, nor the airy titter Jen remembered from when they were young, but a full, throaty guffaw. "OH! OH! HAAA! HEEE!" Brigid's legs, which had been bent at the knee, pressing against Jen's ass, suddenly flew up, clearly pulling Jack into her, because his weight suddenly doubled on atop Jen, and she found herself squeezed between two coming lovers, one bellowing obscenities, the other laughing like a madwoman.

They collapsed, breathless, to the bed.

• •

Jen didn't remember falling asleep. As they'd all lain there, recovering from their exertions, as they'd climbed blindly together beneath the covers, as Jack and Brigid fell quickly to snoring on either side of her, she'd found her mind bouncing among so many subjects — *What the hell do we think we're doing? Did one of us Banish the candles? Of course Jack liked fucking Brigid's tight cunt, how could he not, but did he like hers better…? Is there blood all over…? Do I taste that amazing, or was it only because it was Jack too? Is that how threesomes work, and if so, shouldn't being the one in the middle be more… **more?***

She must have drowsed off though — as her lovers had — because she came to to find herself in a habitual sleeping position: on her knees once more, her forehead against the mattress between Jack's pillow and Brigid's, her ass in the air...

Her hand between her legs. Playing with herself. *They told me,* she thought.

But it wasn't the friction of her fingers moving up and back over her clit that had woken her. No. A pair of fingers much longer and thinner than her own were pressing themselves against the mouth of her cunt. Another set, much larger even than the first, were teasing her sensitive ass. And two more hands-worth were sliding along her ribs. At the same, magical moment, two fingers delved deep into her pussy and another slid into her butt, while two hands found her aching, humming nipples and *squeezed...*

As orgasm flooded through her, all that Jen could think was, *Must be dreaming.*

Panting, she flopped to the bed.

Lips found either cheek. *"Love you,"* said a pair of voices, and then sleep embraced Jen like Death itself, and all was dark.

9 — Isosceles

No!

Jen felt Jack's warmth slipping away from her, as she did so many mornings. Blinking to find only pre-dawn darkness, she murmured, as she always did, "God. Don't go."

This morning didn't feel the same, though. The darkness… was different. Not their house. And though Jack had slipped out of the bed, a pair of legs was still tangled in hers. Soft, smooth legs. And soft, round breasts, pressing against Jen's back and then retreating.

She heard Jack's gruff morning voice. "Got to get in to see if Forensics have traced any of the evidence we collected yesterday."

"If you stay," murmured a low, breathy voice from Jen's dreams, "we could fuck again." Thin, long, warm fingers meandered along Jen's belly.

Jack was silent.

"How could you walk away from an offer like *that*, Phalen?" Jen asked, as images of all of the previous day's events washed across her mind's eye as if she'd been dumped into an over-full scrying bowl, or some really lurid porn video. Sex. And Brigid. And sex. And sex. "Two naked women in your bed?"

He grunted, a kind of chuckle. "Guess I'll have to finish up quick so I can get back here."

Jen was about to pout and plead, but Brigid beat her to it by simply saying, "Please."

In the breathiest, sexiest voice imaginable. Right in Jen's ear.

Funny. Mornings, Jen was usually more inclined to snuggle in bed for a while than to go straight to boffing. Maybe after a pee and a shower. But that *sound…*

"I'll try," said Jack, his voice low and strained in a way that let Jen know that Brigid's plea had affected him in exactly the same way. He was briefly silhouetted in the doorway — instantly recognizable even though he was just a black smudge against the slightly less black rectangle — before he turned and his footsteps echoed up from Brigid's room, and he was gone.

"Mmm," said Brigid, buzzing Jen's earlobe.

"Mmm," answered Jen, and pulled Brigid's arm tight beneath her breasts. She felt her friend's soft curves flowing against her bony spine and shoulders. Jen sighed, warm and content. "You're really here. Feels like a dream."

"Hmm," hummed Brigid, and then murmured, "I'm not sure that I understand what you mean?"

"No?"

Brigid's long fingers cupped themselves around Jen's left breast. "Well, sometimes people say that when they mean that some something is quite lovely. And sometimes they mean that things are very odd. Is that what you meant?"

Jen snorted, the sound seeming unnaturally loud in the dark. "A part of both I suppose. Not *odd*... just.... I mean, last night was a first for me too, you know. I'd never had sex with another woman. Or with two people at once, if it comes to that."

"No." It sounded as if Brigid were smiling.

Jen twisted in her friend's embrace so that they were belly to belly, legs still intertwined, breasts overlapping. "Was it what you thought it would be? Last night?"

Brigid's heartbeat seemed to slow as she considered the question. "No."

"I..." A thickness filled Jen's middle. "Damn. I'm so sorry, Brigid."

"Sorry? Why?"

"Well, I wanted — we both did, Jack and I, we wanted your first time to be magical."

"Oh." Brigid's lips found Jen's, evaporating the weight. "It was that. It was magical in every sense that I can imagine." Kissing Jen again, Brigid let her leg slide up between Jen's thighs until it rested against Jen's vulva, still sticky from the previous evening.

As Brigid's skin slid along her cunt, Jen felt the labia open, moisten. Her breath caught. Could she really *still* be horny? *No Jack here, this morning. Just me and Brigid. And I'm still....*

"Yes, it was quite astonishing, and it felt very, very nice, but it wasn't anything like what I had anticipated. And you were there, of course, which I think I would always have wanted if I had known it were possible."

Jen laughed.

The tip of Brigid's tongue painted a line along the edge of Jen's chin. "I think maybe that my ideas about losing my virginity may have been colored by my... my father's theories about the druids and the effects of letting the blood of a magical being at night."

Jen held her friend, pulling her close, waiting. When Brigid remained silent, Jen squeezed Brigid's ass — Francesca's handiwork still draping perfectly, though there were some stiff spots. "How are you feeling?"

"Actually," Brigid murmured, the fingertips on one hand tracing Jen's ribs while those on the other seemed to be trying to find the absolute edge of the areola on one of Jen's breasts, "I must say that I am finding that my sense of touch is quite enhanced."

"I'm glad," said Jen with a shivering chuckle, "but what I meant was —" She'd meant many things: *Have you realized yet that your mother's dead? Are you still not sure what decade you're in? Did having sex with Jack — with me — leave you as confused as it's left me?* Instead she asked the most pertinent, banal question on her mind: "Are you sore?"

"A bit." The fingers at Jen's breast began to count the bumps on that nipple, which grew and increased as the counting continued. "But it is a nice kind of sore."

"I know what you mean."

"You do? How nice." Then Brigid's other hand brushed along the outside of the unattended breast and began to play with it.

Then they kissed, nibbling and touching and embracing there on the O'Danans' bed, and Jen was fairly sure that they didn't drift back to sleep, but when they finally came up for air, there was a faint dawn light in the room, washing Brigid's face pink. A pink ghost. "Jen?"

God. "Hmm?"

Brigid squeezed her legs together and rocked her pelvis against Jen's hip. "Do you and Jack often pretend to be other people while you are fucking?"

"Uh, no." *Jack's Brigid voice as he lapped at my —* "Never before yesterday. It... In a way, it felt like we were Summoning you. Does that make sense?"

Brigid nodded, her nose sliding along Jen's freckled bump. "I suppose, in way, that you *were* Summoning me. I am very glad that you did." Jen could just make out the smile crinkling the corners of those enormous, luminous eyes.

"Me too." They kissed again, and Brigid began undulating her pelvis against Jen's thigh again, which caused her leg to rock over Jen's cunt and back, and they began to press together... It reminded Jen of dry humping — the way she had Jack and Tony before they'd fucked, even with Michael. But of course then they'd all been clothed, and being teen boys, the guys had come almost immediately, before Jen had gotten more than a tingle of excitement. This... The texture of Brigid's skin was smoother than the silk that still encased her tits, which began to bounce gently against Jen's chest, and the feeling of Brigid's open cunt sliding along Jen's own leg was... Jen couldn't think of a word to describe it.

She stopped trying.

After a while — long enough that Jen began to work up a sweat — Brigid stopped. The change in rhythm actually sparked a small flutter of an orgasm in Jen, and she blinked at the wide, open face in front of her.

Brigid's face, washed in the now golden light of morning, was mottled red. "I want to fuck you."

"Please."

"But just like last night, I don't think that it would be right for you to fuck me."

"*Brigid*," groaned Jen.

Brigid disengaged, and Jen groaned again, reaching up to try to pull the lush form of her lover back to her. Brigid, however, was already at the far side of the bed, retrieving Jen's wand. She tapped the edges of her stained but still sexier-than-hell nightie just above each nipple and over her crotch, and the silk slid down her white, smooth body, revealing a number of small marks that the previous night's play had left. Jen began to move forward, moved by an irrational impulse to kiss the marks away — realizing even as she did that she'd most likely only make the marks worse — but Brigid held up a hand. "Lie down, please."

Unsure where this was going, Jen frowned, but followed Brigid's directions. Brigid crawled up and straddled Jen's midsection. "Lift your head, please."

Jen did; Brigid ran the nightie behind Jen's head and then across Jen's face, so that she couldn't see. The scent of sex was overpowering. Jen's breath, which hadn't slowed much, sped up again. "Brigid?"

"I'm afraid that I sent her down to speak with my marshals," said an airy approximation of a low, gruff voice.

Jen couldn't help it — she laughed. Between the silliness and the irony and the terror that she was about to have sex with Brigid — no Jack this time except in their imaginations — she laughed as no one but

Brigid had ever been able to make her do. "Oh, Jack," she giggled. "I'm so glad you're back!" And she reached up to pull Brigid to her, but Brigid stopped her hands.

"Hmm." Brigid sat there for a moment, holding on to Jen's wrists. "You seem to like playing with my breasts as much as I like playing with yours, but then this won't work. Put your arms above your head, please."

Again, Jen complied — laughter still bubbling, so that her belly bounced against Brigid's round bottom — and Brigid wound the rest of nightie around Jen's arms, tapping the ends and the place where it crossed in front of Jen's eyes so that she was effectively blinded and bound.

Oh, yes, Jen thought, still laughing, though other impulses were fluttering through her middle as well, *yes, this is a game that Jack would like….*

The first time that they'd tied each other up, it had been Jen's idea. It was when Jonathon, their second, was about one, and their sex lives had fallen into a routine — when they could even manage to find the energy. So one night, when Jack had come home after the boys were both asleep, Jen had managed to blindfold herself and tie herself to their bed with their old school ties. When he'd actually come into the room at first he'd been shocked into silence, but then he'd come over and kissed —

Soft, smooth lips touched the inside of Jen's ankle.

"Brigid!"

"You're not supposed to call me that," she whispered up from Jen's calf. "You're supposed to call me *Jack.*"

"Do I have to?"

"Yes."

"Oh, fine," Jen huffed, an exasperated snort of a laugh. "Can't believe you're so horny so soon, *Jack.* After me and Brigid fucked you silly last night."

"Well," answered the voice, almost entirely airy now that Jen had forced Brigid to think again, "you are very sexy. And so I want to fuck you very much."

"Want to fuck you too," Jen grunted, trying to pull Brigid up to her with her legs, wishing she could use her arms — but after all, a competitive flier learned to control her broom without her hands.

Taking the hint, Brigid began to climb up Jen's body.

"Didn't you think Brigid was fucking sexy last night, *Jack?* Didn't you love how she tasted when we were licking her clit? Wasn't it amazing how hard her nipples got when you tweaked them while you were fucking her tight, sweet pussy?"

Brigid whimpered, and began rocking her pubic bone against Jen's clit; Jen had to stifle a groan before she could continue. "You know what I want to do, *Jack*? While you're fucking her, while you're pushing that beautiful cock of yours into her, I want to lick her. I want to lick her clit while you're fucking, I —"

Brigid's mouth clamped onto Jen's, and Jen triumphed in the feeling of her girlfriend's soft, undeniably female body pressing hard against her own.

One of Brigid's hands found Jen's breast while the other grabbed spastically at Jen's ass, trying to pull their pelvises even more tightly together. Again, Jen was reminded of grinding sessions she'd had as a teen. This was infinitely more satisfying: the ripple of Brigid's amazing tits against her own chest, the grind of Brigid's pubis was sending a flame through her body that she knew she had rarely experienced, and definitely never while fully clothed with a scrawny teenaged boy.

Yes, infinitely more satisfying — for Jen, at least. Brigid, her tongue frantically searching Jen's mouth, was moaning in frustration.

"Wait," Jen suggested. She began to move one of her legs beneath and then between Brigid's, so that each was rubbing herself against the other's thigh.

Then Brigid broke the kiss and the dry-humping and it was Jen's turn to feel frustrated. "I have an idea," said Brigid, and turned so that their bodies were at a right angle, their crotches pressed together. Brigid began to rock her pelvis again — but this time their clits slid against each other. "*Shit*!" hissed Brigid, and Jen could only agree; quickly that flame exploded into fireworks, and it was Jen's turn to scream obscenities.

Orgasm screamed through her, leaving her panting, feeling empty, like a bell that's done tolling.

Bell...

Brigid kept sliding her clit over Jen's. If anything her pace was quickening

"Brigid?"

"Hmm?" She sounded as if she might be hyperventilating.

"Was that... the doorbell?"

"Door — ?" whined Brigid.

A low, resonant tone rang from the ground floor.

"*Shite,*" Brigid groaned again, "*just... just —* "

"Brigid, sweetheart. We need to stop. We need to see who that is. Together. It might be an emergency. Or —" *It might be whoever gave you that egg.*

"Oh," said Brigid, somehow both breathy and breathless. "Yes, that is true." She slid away from Jen and onto the floor; Jen could hear her footsteps walking toward the stairs.

"Um... Bri?"

"Hmm?"

"Could you let me loose, please?"

"Oh," said Brigid, her voice even as usual, "of course." Jen felt a tap at either of her elbows and at the bridge of her nose. The nightie-*cum*-restraint fell limply away. "There."

Jen sat up, feeling another small tremor flutter through her. The room was brighter, a golden slash of sunlight running across the O'Danans' bedroom from the bathroom to the far wall. She rolled to the side of the bed where she'd left her pyjamas on the floor the night before. As she stood, about to put them on, she realized that Brigid was once again heading toward the stairs.

"Brigid?"

"Hmm?"

"Clothes." Jen grabbed Brigid's air-bleached yellow pyjama tops and tossed them to her.

Brigid caught them, but blinked down.

"Don't want just anyone seeing what Jack and I got to see, after all," Jen said, pulling on her own togs.

"Oh, yes, I suppose not," Brigid said, looking very much as if her mind were somewhere far away — tracking Cacodaemons or — more likely — still thinking about the not-yet-finished session they'd just abandoned.

"I promise, I'll help you finish."

"Finish?" Brigid's face poked through the neck of the pyjamas, the eyes even more severely unfocussed than usual.

Grabbing her wand from the bed, Jen hooked her arm through her playmate's, kissed her, and pulled her toward the stairs. "Come. Orgasm"

"Oh. That would be very nice."

"Good. I think so too."

When they reached the front door — Brigid having retrieved her own wand from her room on the way — the bell tolled again, loudly enough to make Jen's teeth vibrate. "Jesus, that's a racket!"

"The walls are all very thick, and Daddy's workshop was below ground. Daddy didn't want people to be able to sneak away."

"Okay." Wand at the ready, Jen peered through the peephole. A familiar, gormless face peered back. Smiling in relief, Jen opened the door. "Good morning, Albert."

Al Jenkins, one of Jack's junior marshals, filled the doorway, poised to ring the doorbell again. "Oh. Mrs. Phalen." He seemed to be staring anywhere but at her face.

Brigid pointed her wand at Jenkins's chest. "What is the name of the sister of the woman with whom you had a date last night?"

Jenkins blinked at Brigid, dumbfounded, and Jen was about to say that those sorts of precautions weren't needed any more when she realized that, in fact, Brigid was right to question the marshal's identity. The habits of the war felt as if they had belonged to another life.

"Damn. Er, begging your pardon, miss. Ma'am." Shaking his head as if to clear it, Jenkins stared down at his feet and muttered, "Um, guess you mean Mrs. Williams. Maya."

Frowning slightly, Brigid lowered her wand and stepped back to give the tall man room to enter. Once he was in, she favored him with her vaguest smile. "It is a pleasure to meet you, Deputy Jenkins. Rhea was talking about you last night. I'm Brigid O'Danan."

"I, uh, met you. Or, um, saw you. Thanks." Jenkins continued to fill up the doorway, staring downward as if he were trying to perform a mind-reading spell on the threshold. "And Rhea stood me up."

"That's too bad," said Jen, patting Jon on a shoulder like a block of granite. He flinched. *God, hope he couldn't hear us...* "Come on in, we'll start some tea."

"Thanks, Mrs. P, but I'm on duty. N'koto and I are maintaining perimeter security."

"Of course," Jen said, "thanks. So, what can we do for you?"

Nodding, looking slightly relieved, he finally looked up — though he still seemed to be studiously avoiding eye contact. "I'm sorry to have... um... woken you. But the post office just delivered a couple of hundred letters and packages. Most of 'em are addressed to, erm, Miss O'Danan here, and most of 'em are the kind of trash that usually shows up: scammers, requests for interviews — beginning your pardon, Mrs. P. A few of the rest are on the list Mr. P. left, and we wanted to know if it was okay to send those through."

"Oh," said Brigid, "that would be lovely. Who would want to write us?"

"You'd be surprised, miss," said Jenkins, blushing, and Jen found herself wondering if the young marshal had ever seen quite so much of a naked girl before viewing Brigid's petrified form the previous day.

"Hey, Bri," said Jen, "you've got stationary and stuff, right?"

Brigid nodded.

"Why don't you bring it down. I'll start breakfast."

"Lovely," said Brigid, turning and skipping up the stairs.

Jenkins's eyes nearly bugged out of his head; Jen turned and saw that the canary top on Brigid's disappearing form barely covered her wonderful ass.

Jen patted Jenkins's shoulder again. "Thanks. And Rhea had a, um, family emergency last night. I'm sure she didn't mean to stand you up."

"No, ma'am," sighed the young man. "She sent an owl to that effect, ma'am."

"In any case, thanks so much for getting up so early to guard the house."

"Just doing my duty, ma'am," he said, snapping off a crisp salute. Before he turned, however, he began to blush again and to smile. "Gosh. If it were up to me, Mrs. P., I'd've probably not had any sleep at all last night."

Jen laughed. *Maybe he's not quite so innocent after all.* "Well, maybe if you call Doctor Levy, you can see about ruining tonight's sleep!"

He grinned and dipped his head, turning even redder, and then marched across the O'Danans' yard, back to where Jessamyn N'koto was evidently holding the mailman at bay.

10 — Proof

As they ate the sausages and eggs that Jen had made, Jen sorted through the mail while Brigid worked her way through the morning *Iris-Intelligencer* — as always, reading from the back to the front. She made comments about everything that had changed — higher prices, the planned expansion of Sundown Valley (a risky proposition, giving the magical instability of the land surrounding the town, the racing results (most of which Jen had written before her day off), Felicia Avaya speaking calmly and calmingly about the latest political crisis in Washington.

All the while, a twenty-year-old picture of Brigid herself, taken just after the Battle of the Mountain, smiled from the front page — her photographic self, which looked scarcely younger than the young woman behind the paper, seeming to be trying to read the article below her. **LONG-LOST WAR HERO FOUND** screamed the banner over her head — Aphra hadn't even changed the headline that Jen had written. That *never* happened.

Most of the correspondence was for Brigid — friends from the old days, the O'Danans' family lawyer, Jim Fuchs. Jen had three letters: one from her editor demanding that the follow-up be on her desk by noon; one from Gabe, and one from Tommy Kamiyama, Jen's nephew.

"Brigid?"

"Hmm?" She was reading the finance section — not a subject that Brigid had ever shown any interest in, but she seemed fascinated.

"Rhea's going to be by to check on you around noon." Her note had been folded inside of Gabe's; apparently, they'd had a debriefing of sorts already that morning.

"Maybe she could speak with marshal Jenkins then too."

Jen smiled. "Maybe she could. And Gabe wants to know if it's all right for him and Lyndsey to come over this evening."

"Oh. Yes, I think that would be nice." Brigid flipped to the front page and blinked down at the picture of herself.

"Sorry about the photo." Jen looked down at the postscript to Gabe's letter, in Cynthia's neatest writing, which wasn't very neat at all: *Please may we come to we want to meet Bri Ms. O'Danan so much may we please come please?* — *Cynthia Brigid Phalen*

"Hmm?" Brigid glanced up from the paper. "Oh, the photograph is fine. It is odd to be reading about oneself in the newspaper when one hasn't been attacked by demons."

A nervous laugh escaped Jen's throat. "Yeah. I guess. I wrote that last night, before... Before you'd been revived."

"Yes," said Brigid and smiled. "You always did write well, if rather to the point. And I think it is probably just as well that you cut out the part about my yabos."

"Right. Probably." Jen found that it was even harder after twenty years to tell when Brigid was joking. "Listen, there's two more things. Cynthia and the boys... Our children would like to come down with Gabe. They want to meet you. Desperately."

"Oh," blinked Brigid. "Of course. I should love to meet them."

Jen nodded, not sure why she felt suddenly jealous of her time with Brigid. Well, it would be wonderful to see Cindy, Eddie, and Jon. "And the last: the new Summoning professor really wants to meet you. Addie's a friend of Tommy's."

"Tommy?" Brigid's eyebrows screwed up.

"Tommy? My nephew?"

"Tommy...?" Brigid blinked rapidly, and Jen realized that, to Brigid, Tommy was still a toddler, bouncing off of walls. "Oh. Oh."

"Er, yeah. Hank's son."

"He... He is older than I, now."

"Well..." Jen considered this. It gave her the beginnings of a headache. "I suppose it depends on how you look at it. But, yeah. He and Sally just got engaged."

"*Sally?*" Brigid's eyes enlarged alarmingly. Sally Beauchamp hadn't been out of diapers when Brigid disappeared.

"Yes." Jen let her friend absorb all of that. "Anyway, Addie, Professor Schuler's granddaughter, his successor — she's a good friend of theirs. And apparently she's really anxious to meet you. And Tommy remembers you very clearly and would love to see you again."

"I see." Brigid's eyes remained huge and her complexion pallid.

"I can tell them you need time —"

"No, I should love to see them," said Brigid. Her tone was calm and airy as usual, but her face still bore signs of shock. "I think maybe that would make all of this seem a little more real."

"More than seeing me and Jack gone old and fat?" joked Jen, wondering where the bitterness was coming from.

"You are neither of you old nor fat." Now Brigid began to smile. "You are quite beautiful. It is as if you were the fulfillment of everything that you had always promised to become."

"Thanks," said Jen, feeling warmth flowing into her cheeks and to her crotch.

"And I believe that I am qualified to judge, since I have seen all of each of you that there is to see."

Still blushing, Jen laughed. "True."

"Fucking seems to have the most remarkable way of making you feel very present and at the same time to make the world seem very far away. Has that been your experience?"

"I suppose."

"Hmm. Maybe it is just my inexperience."

Jen reached across the table and grasped the long, white fingers of her friend and lover. "Brigid. Sweetie. I promise you, Jack and I are just as blown away by what happened last night as you are. Neither of us has ever done anything like that. It was amazing."

"Oh?" Brigid sounded vaguely distracted as usual, but her wide eyes brightened, and Jen could feel answering tears in her own. *Fuck.* "How nice."

"*'Nice'* doesn't even begin to describe it."

At that, Brigid smiled. "Would *'fucking fantastic'* come closer?"

"Yes, Brigid." Jen found herself grinning through tears. *Fucking fantastic fucking....* Pulled like iron shavings to a loadstone, Jen leaned across the letters, across the forgotten *Iris-Intelligencer*, and kissed Brigid, kissed her hard, and deep, feeling the love, gratitude, and desire growing as it passed back and forth between them.

Just at the point where the flame had almost consumed Jen again, Brigid pulled back.

Jen groaned, grabbing at the retreating pajama tops.

The object of her desire, however, took a step back, the habitual stoned-looking smile back on her insufferable face — though not without red blossoms of passion spreading across the pale skin, it gratified Jen to notice. "Jen?"

Jen grunted, squeezing her thighs together, feeling as if she finally understood the pained look on her boyfriends' faces when she'd told them it was time to stop.

"You promised to help me finish what we started upstairs this morning."

The sound that welled up from Jen's throat this time had to be more properly classified as a growl.

"Well," said Brigid, her smile expanding, "I think that we should answer the mail quickly and I can help you write an update to that article."

Now Jen's groan was one of disappointment. "Brigid —"

"And then, what I should like very much... that is, if you would like to...?" Brigid looked down, her expression bashful, incredible as that was to consider.

"*Brigid.*"

She looked back up, eyebrows raised hopefully. "I should like it if you tied me up to my bed and if... *Jack* were to go down to me."

"Hnh." Jen looked down at the pile of paper and paper that they'd crumpled in their enthusiasm. "Okay."

"So, whom should we write first," Brigid asked brightly as she sat once more, her still-erect nipples seeming to call to Jen from across the table, "Gabe and your children? I am very much looking forward to meeting your children."

"*Hnh.*"

• •

Once the correspondence had all been taken care of, and Brigid had helped Jen write the article — and Jen noted what a pleasure it was to write with Brigid, for all that both of them were desperate to get it done as quickly as possible, Jen ran out to the deputies outside — the mailman was still waiting — and sent all of those words off with the mail and out of her mind. She locked the front door and all but sprinted up the stairs to Brigid's bedroom, her mind full of images from the previous night, images from that morning, images from their girlhood, lying side-by-side on that bed, each pleasuring herself, but —

The sight of Brigid bound naked and blindfolded on that bed swept thoughts of childhood far away. Brigid's was not a girl's body any more, not by any stretch of even Brigid's prodigious imagination. Hers was a woman's body, and it inspired feelings in Jen that she couldn't put a name to — except that it was soft and warm and electric, like the feeling of their breasts bouncing together or their cunts.

"Hello, Jack," said Brigid. "I asked Jen if you would get down on me. Would you — ?"

Jen's mouth found Brigid's cunt before she could ask any further, striking Brigid, for once, speechless.

The taste of Brigid's cunt, the smooth wetness of it, Brigid's voice, high and airy, the scent of her arousal, the sight of those gorgeous yabos quivering — Jen wanted this. *SHE* wanted it. She wanted to give this to Brigid, and to receive it. She felt greedy and gratified to deliver such pleasure to this amazing, beautiful, astonishing woman. And so as Brigid reached and tumbled over the pinnacle and screamed, "JEN!" it pleased her far more than she could comprehend.

She crawled up Brigid's still-trembling body, felt the now-familiar, always astonishing shock of their breasts flowing over each other, and found Brigid's mouth searching blindly for hers.

"Brigid," Jen sobbed, body pressing against her lover's even as tears made her whole world wet, "want to fuck you, love you so much, want to fuck you, me, you, not Jack, just —"

Brigid answered by throwing her legs over Jen's butt and squeezing Jen as if trying to erase any border between them.

• •

Afterward, after they had made love, and after Jen had finally released Brigid from her bonds, they lay tangled in each other like skeins of thread on Brigid's bed.

Brigid hadn't laughed when she'd come. She hadn't even giggled. She'd just screamed Jen's name again, and howled.

Jen could feel their pulses slowing in tandem, could feel each of them catching her breath.

"I love you, too," Brigid whispered, her face slick with sweat and tears.

When the doorbell tolled once more, Jen wanted to scream at whoever it was to go away, but Brigid was the sensible one this time: "It might be Jack."

And so, unsteadily, they both got up and put on clothing that reeked of sex nearly as much as they did. "Stay here," Jen said, remembering that her job was to protect Brigid, to keep Brigid safe.

"All right," answered the redhead.

As Jen walked away, however, she could feel a thread pulling taut between them, and she knew then that something had changed. Stumbling down the stairs, legs rubbery, she felt as if she had been the one to wake into a strange new world. And she wondered how she could explain this to Jack.

It was not Jack at the door, however; it was Rhea, coming to check on Brigid as she'd said she would. Jen felt a sense of guilty relief that it wasn't her husband — she had so much to digest just now before she could even begin to talk to the man she loved about it.

So bewildering. All this love.

Shaking her head, Jen invited Rhea up the stairs. "How's Maya and Tony?" she whispered.

"Like you'd expect." Rhea shrugged. "I knew I'd ignite a shitstorm, telling them, but I knew I needed to be the one to tell them."

"Yeah. Still. Ouch."

"Tell me about it. Maya all sure that Tony would leave her. Tony totally flogging himself because Maya actually thought he'd do that, and because he'd given up on Brigid, and because someone other than Maya could make him feel that way. I was there until five this morning, and they were still veering between yelling at themselves and yelling at each other." Rhea's face, which was uncharacteristically somber, lightened into a smirk. "Finally told them not to commit murder or suicide without consulting me first, but I was going to bed. That shut them up long enough to get me out of the apartment."

"Tony...?" whispered Jen, and Rhea winced, which was all of the answer that Jen needed. As they began to ascend the stairs to the second floor, Jen could see her own face on the ceiling, framed by the stairwell. "Well," she said, trying to change the mood, "I told Jenkins you'd had a family emergency, and he didn't seem to mind."

That brought a broader smirk to Rhea's face. "Yeah. I offered to give him a blowjob just now by way of apology, but he got all flustered and told me he was on duty."

Jen laughed.

"Mostly," continued Rhea with her own chuckle, "I did it to see him go all red. Boy that big blushing, that's quite a sight, believe me."

"Hello, Rhea," said Brigid, leaning demurely against the headboard she'd been thrashing against not fifteen minutes before. "It is lovely to see you again."

"You, too, babe," said Rhea, sitting on the bed.

Jen was very conscious that the whole room was full of the smell of their fucking — wasn't sure that the sounds of their cries weren't still echoing around the walls of the house.

"I just need to give you a quick follow-up physical," Rhea said. She gave Jen a significant glance. "Jen, would you mind — ?"

It was the same routine as when the kids had cursed themselves. Jen nodded. "I'll give you some privacy. Would you guys like me to make a fresh pot of tea?"

"That would be great," said Rhea, while Brigid merely smiled as if the sun had taken up residence in her belly.

As Jen walked down the stairs, she forced herself to look at what she had been avoiding all morning: Jack.

She loved Jack. She had loved him for all of her adult life. Since she was sixteen, for God's sake. They had a rich, mostly wonderful life together. They had three mostly wonderful children. He still made her happy — most of the time. The huge majority of the time. As yesterday had proved, he was still more than capable of pleasing her, in bed or out.

He was Jack. He loved her and she loved him.

But Brigid....

What had come over Jen? She hadn't felt so carried away in bed since... Since forever. At least it seemed so now. And it wasn't just the sex... But, *God*. The *sex*.

Jen was blindly pouring the boiling water into the tea, her mind anywhere but in this kitchen when Rhea came down the stairs. Blinking away the jumble of thoughts, she covered the teapot and turned. "So, clean bill of health?"

Rhea was looking at the floor, her mouth a straight line. "Brigid is... physically fit."

"That's for sure," Jen said, attempting a joke.

Rhea, however, didn't smile.

"Rhea?" Anxiety began to flood into Jen's chest.

"Brigid's fine. " Taking a deep breath, Rhea squared her shoulders, but her eyes still didn't meet Jen's. "Jen, I have a couple of things I want to ask, okay?"

Though the fear was no longer blossoming, it was still there, cold now, and heavy. "Sure. Rhea?"

"You've... You stayed here last night, didn't you?"

"Of course. Jack and me, both of us. What's going on, Rhea? You're frightening me."

Now Rhea looked up, a note of apology leavening her somber expression. "You didn't leave at all, did you? You slept here?"

The image of the previous night, of the three of them on Brigid's parents' bed, of waking to find Jack's finger pressing into her ass while Brigid's searched Jen's cunt... "Uh, yeah."

"And... Jack. Did he stay here last night too?" Rhea looked as if the question cost her a lot.

"What? Well, yeah, both of us. I told you. We stayed up in the room on the top floor."

"And did Jack... Jen. Did you leave the two of them alone at all, Jack and Brigid?"

"*What?*" No, no, Jen hadn't left Brigid's side except after she'd gone to bed in her own room — before she interrupted Jack and Jen and — "No."

"No? Jen, are you sure?"

"Yes, Rhea. I was with Brigid all last night, and Jack never left the bed till he left for the Ministry just before dawn. What — ?"

Rhea came closer. "Jen, I.... Jen, when I examined Brigid yesterday, she was... *virgo intacta.*"

Comprehension dawned. Rhea thought that *Jack* — ? "Oh. Oh, God."

"I'm so sorry, Jen. I... I want to *kill* Jack, really."

Jen fought to hold down the laughter that was fighting its way up her throat. *Of course Rhea would notice.* "Rhea. It wasn't Jack, wasn't just Jack. It was both of us."

"*What?*" Now it was Rhea's turn to stare incredulously.

"It..." It suddenly occurred to Jen that Rhea would understand, Rhea who had slept with men and with women, and probably with both, and maybe she could help Jen understand. "It was the three of us, and it —"

"*Jen.*" Rhea's eyes pierced Jen. "Do you have any idea...? That young woman is in an *incredibly* vulnerable state! I can't believe... the two of you, Jack a fucking *marshal*, for God's sake! *How* could you take advantage of *that poor girl's* — ?"

"Rhea, I swear," Jen gasped, guilt and shame replacing fear in her chest, "we wouldn't, I —"

"It wasn't like that," said a calm, airy voice from the stairs, and both Jen and Rhea spun to face it.

Brigid was standing there, utterly naked but for the emerald choker at her throat. Her skin, which had been flawless when they had revived her the day before, was marked with small bruises, each of which brought another clear memory of shameful ecstasy to Jen's tortured mind.

"Brigid," Rhea said, once again looking at the floor. "You know that you're in a difficult —"

"Yesterday," Brigid said, as forcefully as she ever said anything, "my yesterday, that is, yesterday twenty years gone by, Tony had promised to come and finally to take my virginity. To fuck me. I had wanted it so much, for so long, you see, and so when I woke to discover that Tony... was no longer available, that, I will admit, left me feeling rather unsettled. And so when I went up to Jack and Jen's room after they had thought I'd gone to sleep, I went up and they... They were fucking, and it..." Brigid flushed, sending a *frisson* through Jen. "I asked them to. To take my virginity. It was very nice."

Very nice. Very interesting. *Indeed.*

Rhea shook her head. "Brigid —"

"They did not take advantage of me, Rhea. If anything, I took advantage of them. Jack had never had sex with anyone but Jen. Jen had never had sex with a woman. They gave me what I needed because they care for me."

Jen rasped, "We love you, Bri."

Brigid smiled, a crescent moon of a smile this time. "And I love you both too, Jen. But Rhea, if anything has helped me join the present, *this* present, it was their gift to me. They have not abused me. Not at all."

Blinking, Rhea looked from Brigid to Jen and back. "Jesus Christ." Then a very Rhea-like grin warmed her face, and she laughed. "Damn, Brigid. One hell of a way to pop your cherry."

"Cherry?" Brigid's wide forehead furrowed.

"Lose your virginity," mumbled Jen, feeling drained.

"Oh. Yes," Brigid said, face relaxed again. "I was very fortunate."

Now Rhea laughed. "No kidding. Lucky Brigid!" She turned and gave Jen a hug and whispered into her ear, "Lucky Jen too!"

Jen nodded, unable to speak, and returned Rhea's hug. Her focus, however, was on Brigid, who stood unselfconsciously on the stairs, naked, red hair tangled, looking like a sex dream, a love goddess.

Stepping back, Rhea held Jen by the shoulders. "I'm sorry. I shouldn't have... I just assumed that Jack had —"

"Jack wouldn't."

"No, I know, I think that's why I was so angry, it just didn't seem like him at all. I guess he's still a bit of a hero to me."

"Me too," Jen admitted with a laugh of relief. "Even if he does leave his dirty clothes on the floor."

"I never thought of him as a hero," mused Brigid. "He was too nice, and he liked bacon."

Both Rhea and Jen laughed at that. Together they walked to the foot of the stairs. Jen wondered if Rhea was as lost as Jen in the rise and fall of Brigid's breasts, which were right at eye level. Jen found herself cataloguing the love bites, trying to guess by the size and shape which she herself had given Brigid, and which were Jack's.

Rhea laughed again. "Yeah. Lucky Brigid. Well, my fortunate friend, I pronounce you fully healthy. If you notice anything strange — well, stranger than usual — don't hesitate to call me. I know I'm going to be writing you up for *The Healer*, if that's okay."

"Oh, of course. I should very interested to see the article. Though maybe you shouldn't include the sex."

"Probably not," both Jen and Rhea agreed.

Brigid considered this, and then nodded. "I'm going back up to bed, Jen." She turned and walked back upstairs.

Like Jen, Rhea was speechless at the sight. When the pale, round ass had disappeared, Rhea shook her head again and turned back to Jen. "Lucky Jen. No fucking kidding. And here I thought you and Jack weren't the sharing type."

"Believe me," Jen sighed, "this is as much of a shock to us as it is to you." The two women chuckled together. "Rhea, please, I know I don't need to say it, but please, don't talk to anyone about this. Not even Jack. *Especially* Jack. He'd be mortified."

"Jen, Jen, I'm a doctor. Keeping people's secrets is part of my job." She leaned forward and kissed Jen on the cheek. "This secret will be keeping *me* warm in bed for quite a while, though. Wow."

As Rhea turned to leave, Jen felt a blush sweep over her, and didn't even bother to try to hide it.

Turning at the front door, Rhea winked. "I think I'm going to go see if I can get Al Jenkins to turn that color. It's damned sexy." And with that, she was gone.

What had she been thinking? Because Jen knew that the previous night had been *her* idea — or at least, she had been the one to voice what they were all thinking and to make it real. *Had* she taken advantage of her lovely, lonely friend, lost in time as Brigid was so often lost in space? Would Jack be able to handle the qualms that Jen was sure he would be suffering, the silly boy? And she and Brigid, they had made love, and it had been *amazing*, but how would Jack...?

All thought was banished from her head, however, when she reached the second floor.

Brigid was on the bed, running Jen's wand over her open cunt lips and circling the glistening clitoris that stood out insistently from the lips and Brigid's red thatch. "I was thinking that the first time that I touched you sexually, I only gave you one lick. I should very much like to taste you some more if you would like that."

Jen's turmoil notwithstanding, her body was certain that it *would* like that, thanks very much. Fingers trembling inexplicably, she threw off the clothing that she'd spent far more time out of than in over the past eighteen hours, and joined Brigid on the bed, watching a unicorn on the bedspread gallop around Brigid's butt, disappearing at one cheek only to reappear momentarily at the other. Jen lay down beside her lover and kissed that cheek still lost in its marble whiteness, knowing that it would redden again soon enough. Brigid leaned forward and, without preliminary licked at Jen's privates.

Last night, that long tongue had skyrocketed Jen straight to orgasm. This time it merely sent a geyser of sweet heat up her spine. How many times had she come in the last day? Jen tried to count and got lost somewhere around six or seven or... Well, it didn't really matter. A lot. And yet her body was ramping up to take the dive once more. Amazing.

To keep herself from getting totally lost in the sensation too soon, she began running her hands over Brigid's ass, her legs, her pussy. When the lips there flowered open again, Jen scooted underneath and between Brigid's thighs, pulling that sweet cunt down to her mouth.

"Oh!" sighed Brigid into Jen's own cunt. "Can we do this?"

"We can do," gasped Jen, "whatever we fucking want."

Brigid gave a squeak as Jen sucked Brigid's clit into her mouth. "Oh."

"'S called sixty-nine."

"Huh." Brigid shivered. "Numerolo... Huh."

"'Cause of how the numbers look together."

"Huh."

Jen gave herself over to the closed circuit of pleasure that they were building between them. Trying not to think about how much Jack enjoyed this, wondering if maybe she could eat him while he at Brigid while she ate —

Brigid's mouth detached itself from between Jen's legs, leaving a cool ache. "Hello, Jack," said Brigid. "Is something wrong?"

Jack stood at the top of the stairwell. His cock was in his hand, but his face was dark and full of storm as Jen had not seen it since the morning of Chancellor Spires's death.

11 — Differential

Jack scowled at Jen, at Brigid, where the two had tangled themselves head-to-pelvis on Brigid's bed. But his cock was hard in his hand. "I don't know, Brigid. *Is* something the matter?" He said it to Brigid, but he was staring at Jen.

"No, Jack," Jen said. "Nothing at all."

"Well," sighed Brigid, her breath puffing across Jen's labia and making Jen shiver, "you did say you would come back soon, so we've been keeping busy."

"Is that so?" Jack smiled, though his eyes remained dark.

"Uh-huh," Jen said, reaching out over Brigid's leg and grabbing her husband's erection, hand and all, and pulling him toward her. "Everything's just fine."

And before he could ask anything else, she pulled him into her mouth.

Oral sex had always been a favorite part of Jen and Jack's play together, even in recent years when play had become a bit of a lost art. Each loved using the tongue, the lips, the teeth to pleasure the other. Giving and receiving.

Jen loved the closed circuit of sixty-nine, loved how all-encompassing it was. Jack, however, had always found it difficult to concentrate on doing *anything* while he was being eaten, and so they hadn't done that in years.

Now, however, Brigid brought her mouth back to Jen's cunt and began to explore it, sending flame up through Jen's body, and for the first time she had some sense of what Jack meant. The thick pressure of his cock spreading her mouth — usually something that Jen enjoyed — seemed almost *too* much on top of Brigid's lapping.

She pulled her mouth off of that familiar cock, but continued to stroke it even as she looked up at her husband, who was staring down at her. In the diffuse afternoon light of Brigid's room, his glasses were all but opaque. Kissing the glistening tip of his cock — fighting to keep clarity as Brigid blew lightly on Jen's pussy lips — she whispered huskily, "Was... *Unh...* Was telling Brigid I wanted to... Lick you both while you fucked her."

The eyes were just as unreadable, but Jack shivered.

Jen ran her fingers over Brigid's open cunt lips. Amazing to think that she'd been squeamish about doing that just a day before. "Bri?"

"Hmm?" Brigid hummed against Jen's clit.

"Hnh. Um. You ready for your second fuck, sweetie, or are you still sore?"

"Oh." Brigid disengaged from Jen's pussy, her hair flowing over Jen's thighs and belly. "No, I think I should rather like Jack to fuck me, if he wouldn't mind." Then she went back to licking.

Smiling, Jen peered up at her husband. "Would you mind, dear? Fucking Brigid's tight, sweet pussy while I nibble on you both?" With the hand that had been stroking Jack's cock, she pulled him toward that very tight, very sweet pussy.

"Wait," he grunted — she was shocked that he'd resisted, and began to fall back into panic, but he simply stepped back and dropped his jeans and his boxers to the floor. His shirt and his greatcoat still on, he stepped back to kneel on the bed, and allowed Jen once more to guide him into Brigid's waiting cunt.

It was astonishing to watch that oh-so-familiar erection approach that now-very-familiar cunt, to watch it split the fine lips. Fascinating to see that amazing cock press into that wonderful cave. Exhilarating to hear both of her lovers hiss and then groan.

"I like... this direction... too," sighed Brigid, panting into Jen's crotch.

"Me... *Oh, FUCK!* Me too," said Jack, pressing further in. "Not too... *hard,* Brigid?"

"No," Brigid said after a moment of consideration. "I'm actually finding this rather easier than last night."

Lying beneath them, Jen found herself chuckling. These two were nothing in bed if not entertaining. *And God,* she thought, *are they ever entertaining!* Leaning up, she gave a long lick that ran from Brigid's clit, along the base of Jack's thrusting cock, and onto his balls, which were hanging loose.

"FUCK!" groaned her lovers in unison — ethereal Brigid and taciturn Jack — making Jen grin to herself.

"Like that, do you?" she sighed, and licked them again, evoking more swearing. Jack, who had started out with such restraint, was now pounding into Brigid, his balls sliding along Jen's forehead. Though Brigid's mouth was no longer latched on to Jen's pussy, Jack's thrusts were causing Brigid's whole face to bounce along Jen's crotch, her breasts to bounce and slide across Jen's belly, which actually felt kind of amazing.

Jen went back to lapping at them — it was hard to aim much, but Jack's thrusts kept them moving over her tongue. It must have been working, because soon Brigid's belly began trembling as it flowed over Jen's breasts.

Brigid let out a long sigh; Jen could feel her collapse forward, could feel Brigid's breath against the inside of her thigh. Pushing up on her elbows, Jen got more aggressive about lapping at her girlfriend and her husband.

Jack was swearing, but it was quietly; his balls were still loose, sliding along Jen's forehead. It didn't sound as if he were going to be getting off any time soon. When was the last time that he had come... How many times? Four times in the last day? Five? Jen wasn't sure, but she was fairly sure that, like her, her husband hadn't been so sexually satisfied in a long time. She was pleased and impressed that he'd been able to get so hard — *stay* so hard — but then, as she'd told Brigid that morning, two naked women in your bed would tend to provide *some* inspiration.

Against the inside of Jen's thigh, Brigid's moans were beginning to rise in pitch and volume; Jack's thrusts pushed Brigid's pelvis further up in the air, forcing Jen to press further up on her arms. On either side of Jen's cheeks, Brigid's thighs were vibrating with building tension, rippling as Jack's cock slammed home. Squeezing as if to hold on to the moment — and Jen's head.

Knowing that Brigid was close, and not sure that she could hold on much longer, Jen reached up with her lips and sucked in Brigid's slick clit.

That did it.

Jen was quickly becoming a connoisseur of Brigid's orgasms. This was neither the wall-shaking bellow she'd given when Jen and Jack had both licked her, nor screaming Jen's name as she had earlier that morning, nor the raucous laughter with which she'd punctuated her first fuck. This time, Brigid's release was long and sustained; she let loose a high moan into the flesh of Jen's thigh as her legs and butt tightened to keep Jen and Jack both exactly where they were. The only movement that Jen was aware of for a moment was the rhythmic pulse of Brigid's cunt against Jen's lips, her nose, and Jack's cock.

Then the moment was gone and Brigid went limp and collapsed onto Jen, letting Jack slip out of her. "Oh," said Brigid.

"Um," said Jack, voice higher than usual, the poor boy. Jen could feel the tip of his cock slide along her forehead, trailing moisture, seeking for Brigid's cunt again.

Brigid grunted softly. "Ow."

"Oh. Um."

Jen could hear the tension in her husband's voice, knew that, even having come, and come, and come, they couldn't leave him hanging like this. *Suck him off,* she considered, *or...?*

Then the image flashed into her mind of the fantasy that Jack had told her about the previous night. The fantasy that he'd beat off to all those years ago. Sliding out from under Brigid's still-boneless body, Jen reached up and stroked her husband, which caused his mouth and eyes to close. "Brigid, sweetie?"

"Mmm."

"Think you can sit up? There's something you and I can do for Jack that I think he'll enjoy."

Brigid didn't move, but sighed, "Oh. How nice."

"Yeah. I think so."

Jack grunted. "Jen?"

"Come on, Bri, let's sit you up." Kneeling up, Jen looked down at Brigid, at her back, which was flushed, and at her butt, which was bright from Jack's onslaught. "Come on." Jen helped Brigid sit, pulled her so that Jen was leaning against the headboard with Brigid, lax, between her legs. Jen cupped her hands around her friend's — her lover's — wonderful tits, pressing them together lightly even as she let her fingers play over those amazing nipples. She glanced at her husband.

He was kneeling at the foot of the bed, his eyes boring into Jen's. He knew *exactly* what Jen had in mind.

Jen smiled. "Brigid, sweetheart, do you remember what we told you last night, how Jack used to lie in his bed, stroking that *lovely penis*, and thinking about —"

"About pressing them between my yabos. Yes."

"While I held them." She grinned at her husband. "What a nasty mind you had, Jack. Did it look anything like this?"

"Nowhere near as sexy."

Jen grinned. He might still be angry with them — with her — but he was playing along. "Want to see if these feel as good as you thought?"

He didn't answer, but dropped his coat, moved up and straddled Brigid's waist and Jen's legs, and without preamble thrust his red, dripping penis up between the smooth, firm flesh of Brigid's breasts. *"God!"*

Jen grinned. "Nice?"

Brigid sighed, her head flopped back over Jen's should. "Oh, yes. It feels quite lovely."

Jen bet her earlobe and gloried as Brigid arched, her areolae bristling beneath Jen's fingers, and Jack hissed. "I'm glad it feels lovely. Jack?"

"God." He was picking up the pace of his thrusts. Looking up at him, Jen saw that he was staring down at the two of them, grasping onto the headboard as he leaned over them.

Still grinning, Jen glanced down to where his cock was disappearing and then pushing back up through the yielding mounds of Brigid's breasts, the insides of which were slickening with pre-cum. "Brigid," she whispered.

"Hmm."

"Look down."

Brigid picked her head up slowly and then peered toward where Jack's cockhead was playing peek-a-boo between her tits. *"Mmm"*

"Yeah. *Mmm.* Want to taste it?"

"Oh. May I?"

"Fine with me! Jack?"

"SHIT!"

Jen felt giddy laughter bubble up. "That's a yes, Brigid. Take a lick.

Brigid's long tongue snaked out and, at the top of Jack's up-thrust, lapped at the head of his cock, wetting it even more.

"OH, FUCK!"

Out loud this time, Jen said, "Taste nice?"

"Oh, yes," said Brigid, stopping for a slurp and then continuing, "very interesting." Another slurp. "A bit like mandrake."

"Yeah," said Jen, remembering the smell of Gabe's salve. "Try kissing it."

Brigid let Jack's cockhead slide against her lips.

"AHH! SHIT!"

"Mmm." Brigid hummed. "May I —" Another kiss. " — take it into my mouth —" Kiss. " — like you did?"

"Don't think Jack will mind."

"FUCK NO!"

Jen watched as Brigid opened her lips and that cock that Jen had swallowed hundreds or maybe thousands of times slid for the very first time into another woman's mouth.

"OH! FUCK!"

Jen whispered, "Press your tits together for me, will you, Brigid, sweetie?"

Around Jack's cock, which she was now swallowing rather expertly, Brigid hummed, *"Mmm."* Her hands slid up beside Jen's, taking over.

Jen slid her now-free hands around her husband's clenching buttocks. Leaning her head as far forward as she could, she joined Brigid in licking his swelling erection.

"SHIT! AW, *SHIT! JEN! BRI — ! Brigid!"*

With one hand, Jen reached around and found Jack's testicles, which were quickly tightening as he approached orgasm. Knowing it would send him over the edge, Jen did something she hadn't tried in years: she slid her finger between his butt-cheeks and brushed the puckered hole there.

As she'd guessed, Jack arched back, his cock barely poking out from between Brigid's breasts, and howled, letting loose a surprisingly strong, surprisingly substantial stream of hot jism that sprayed onto both Brigid's face and Jen's own.

"God," gasped Jack, and collapsed off of them and onto the bed.

Bridy as she had been for large portions of the previous day — not quite eighteen hours — Jen began to kiss and lick the cum off of Brigid's cheek, her nose.

Brigid turned in her arms and began lapping like a kitten at Jen's face.

Just at the point where she could feel the flame reigniting — *No. Mustn't. They're done.* — Jen felt Jack slide up her body and whisper something into Brigid's ear.

"Oh. Yes. That would be nice," sighed Brigid into Jen's mouth, and began to lick and nibble her way down Jen's chin and neck.

Jack, as always, was more direct, sliding down and taking Jen's nipple into his mouth.

"Hnh!" The difference between Jack's assertive approach and Brigid's more indirect meander was definitely enough to short-circuit whatever part of Jen's brain was anything like clear.

As soon as Brigid's mouth began to experiment with as many ways as it could of torturing Jen's right breast in the most delicate way imaginable, Jack left the left one, kissing his way down her belly and hip.

Being with one lover was an immersion — all-encompassing, shrinking the universe down to a single point of intersection.

Being with two was envelopment — expanding into their touches and through them out to the edges of the universe.

Holy fuck.

Jack lifted Jen's leg, kissing his way beneath it.

"Uh... Jack...?"

"Shh."

"Uh..." Jen tried to remember why she was feeling guilty. It was there, somewhere, she knew.... "You... don't... have to..."

"Oh, we don't *have* to do anything," murmured Brigid. "We want to go down to you together. Isn't that right, Jack?"

Jen stared down into the dark flame of her husband's gaze.

He pulled on her pubes with his teeth. "Yup."

"Oh... Okay."

And with that, Jack began to lick at her as he had learned to do so masterfully over the years, while Brigid leisurely kissed her way down Jen's tummy and over her hip. At an achingly impossible moment, their tongues met around Jen's clit, and the infinite boundaries of creation beckoned.

• •

"Know why you passed out when we did that to you last night." Jen was tangled in their bodies, feeling the aftershocks of orgasm spark through her still.

"Oh?" Brigid said against Jen's belly. "Yes."

Jen chuckled, petting Brigid's head and Jack's, which lay between her breasts.

He was staring up at her, smiling but eyes still smoldering.

"Jack," Jen said, "I'm so sorry we started without you."

He grunted, his stare just as intense. A small smile lightened his expression, however. "Glad I sent N'Koto and Jenkins away, then."

"Oh. God." *What will Al Jenkins think!* Jesamyn, Jen knew, would keep any opinions she might have firmly to herself. "They... You couldn't hear us, could you?"

"Only once I was coming up the stairs," Jack said. "Thick walls. What time is it?"

"Time?" Jen blinked.

"Yeah." Jack sat up, searching through the coat that he'd shucked.

"You let them go?" asked Brigid, her gaze following Jack remarkably closely — for Brigid anyway.

"Oh. Yeah." Jack pulled his legendary granddad's watch out from the pocket of his greatcoat. "Almost one. We should all take a shower."

A shiver passed through Jen though she wasn't sure why. "Jack?"

"Solved Brigid's case," he said. "We've got some visitors coming in a bit." Then he shook himself, that small smile returning. "That's why I was pissed off when I came in, not because of what you two were up to."

"What is it, Jack?"

He shook his head again. "I promised I'd let him explain. Come on. Let's get cleaned off."

· ·

Maybe it wasn't surprising that, though they showered together, it was a relatively chaste affair, each of them cleaning the previous night's stickiness and that morning's away, doing each other's backs maybe, but no more than might be expected.

Jack's mood continued to make Jen unaccountably nervous, and Brigid was unusually withdrawn. Jen didn't blame her. Whoever was coming, whatever the explanation was, it would make clear why Brigid had lost her mother, her boyfriend and twenty years of her life. It was enough to make anyone think about things a bit.

Jen spelled their clothes clean. She found an outfit for Brigid other than the faded pyjamas and the wonderfully obscene nightie: what was for Brigid a fairly conservative ensemble of a knee-length skirt and a yellow top. Jen pulled one of Brigid's old, hand-knit sweaters over her t-shirt and jeans.

Jack was back in his marshal gear. He had his business face on. "Come on," he said. "Let's go downstairs. They'll be here soon."

"They?" Brigid asked.

"Yeah." More than that he wouldn't say.

They had just reached the kitchen when the doorbell tolled. "I'll get it," Jack said.

Jen took Brigid's hand. "Okay, Bri?"

Brigid nodded abstractedly. When Jen squeezed her hand, Bri shot her a smile that communicated more animal panic than warmth.

"Come in," Jack said, and three figures shuffled through the door: Rhea and the Williamses — Maya and Tony.

Rhea looked guarded. Maya glowered.

Tony was a wreck. Jen hadn't seen him like this in years. Since just after Brigid's disappearance. His skin was — for him — pale and bloodless. He had dark circles under his eyes, which were red and bloodshot. He'd been crying. He'd been drinking again.

Brigid's hand clutched at Jen's.

Jack cleared his throat. "We had put it together this morning —"

"The green and yellow stripes on the Caco — on the Gorgon egg," said Brigid, her voice barely above a whisper. "It was paint, was it?"

Jack nodded.

Jack looked at Brigid, who was as white as she had been when she had been marble the day before, and then at Tony, who swayed next to his wife, who stood with her arms crossed. Rhea had her hands on her sister's shoulders. Again, Jack cleared his throat. "Tony came in and… confessed before we went and talked to him."

Now they all stared at Tony, who was crying. Jen had never seen him cry.

"Tony," said Maya, her voice flat.

Tony shook himself. "Wanted to get it for you, wanted to so badly, Brigid, looked everywhere, knew you'd looked, so I talked to Esau and asked him, you know, to help me find…" Tony broke down, put his head in his hands, and sobbed. "*SO sorry, Bri!*"

Jen looked from Brigid, who was stone-faced, to Tony, who was a red-eyed mess.

Rhea pushed her sister, whose arms were crossed in an increasingly tight knot. With a grunt, Maya went and put her arms around her husband, who collapsed into them.

"He finally told me after Rhea left last night," Maya said. "Said Esau…" She glanced at Jack.

Jack nodded and took over. "Esau Whitworth was always one of the best Summoners in the valley — other than you of course, Brigid, and Professor Schuler, and now his granddaughter Addie. But he was never exactly *careful* about which planes he summoned from. It's how he died — summoning a Greater Duh into a circle he hadn't drawn carefully enough."

"D-duh?" Brigid whispered. Brigid had always loved the eight-eyed spirits — but if anyone had known how dangerous they could be, it was her.

Jack nodded. "In any case, he's paid for his crime. Statute of limitations ran out on Tony's negligence years ago, but there's no such thing on voluntary manslaughter, and selling Tony here a Gorgon egg and telling him it's a Cacodaemon egg is that at the very least."

They all stared at Brigid. Brigid stood like the statue that she had been for two decades.

Still sobbing into Maya's shoulder, Tony cried again, "*So sorry, Bri!* If... I p-painted it so it'd look just like you'd... If I'd *known*... Thought all this time I'd *killed you*, and your mom too, and, oh, God, just wanted to *die...!*"

"Thank you for telling me, Tony," Brigid said, voice low but even. "I think you should leave now."

Tony sobbed again, but it was Maya who answered. "He's been torturing himself for twenty years, Brigid. He's paid for his crime."

Brigid nodded. "Yes. But for me, all of this happened only yesterday. I am afraid that it will be quite a while before I am able to forgive you. Now," she repeated, more firmly, "please leave."

Tony shot her a look of pure shame, but Maya shook her head, and he groaned. Bent, head once more in his hands, he shuffled back out the door.

"He really is sorry," Maya said. "I know that you have no reason to forgive him, but when you can, please, try." When Brigid gave a short nod, Maya followed her husband out the door.

Rhea watched them go and then turned somberly back into the room. "I'm so sorry, Brigid. Are you all right?"

"No," said Brigid, as calm as ever, "I do not think that I am. However, physically I believe that I am perfectly healthy."

Rhea nodded. "I don't know that the same can be said for Tony. Jen, Jack. I'll leave Brigid in your hands. I know you'll take care of her." When they both nodded, she too left, closing the door behind her.

Jen threw her arms around her oldest, youngest friend. "Oh, Brigid."

Brigid stood rigidly in her embrace, even when Jack strode over and hugged her from the other side. "We'll get Whitworth," he muttered. "It's not any consolation, but he'll pay. We don't think it was in any way because it was *you*, if that helps; we think he just wanted to make some gold and sow some havoc."

"Actually, Jack," said Brigid, still staring at the door, "I don't believe that that helps at all." Gently, she disengaged herself, stepping back from them. "I love you both very much, but if you don't mind, I should very much like to go down to my mother's workshop and be alone for a while."

"Brigid —" Jen said, simultaneous with Jack.

"Do not worry. I do not wish to harm myself at all, but I do wish to scream rather loudly and break some things." Brigid nodded. "Yes. I think that I do. And I do not think that I should be able to do what I need to do if you were there with me."

Jen frowned and shot a glance at Jack, who shook his head. He said, "Do you promise to be careful?"

Brigid nodded.

"Do you promise not to do anything to hurt yourself?"

Brigid gave a mild scowl, and then nodded again. "Yes. I think that I can promise that."

"If we give you an hour, do you think that you could do what you need to do in that time?"

"I'm not sure, but that should be enough time to get started."

"All right," said Jack, giving Jen's shoulder a gentle squeeze. "We'll go up to your room. If we don't hear from you by two o'clock, we're going to come down and make sure that you're still okay."

Brigid smiled, stepped forward, and kissed Jack lightly. "Thank you, Jack. Thank you, Jennifer," she added, kissing Jen. Then she turned, spoke her own name, and stepped down into the darkness through the trap door, which she closed behind her.

Her heart in knots, Jen looked at her husband.

He folded her in his arms. "I'm sure she'll be all right, Jen," he said. "She needs the space to grieve, and we need to give her that. And I," he added, walking her to the stairs, "need to spend some time just with my wife. Okay?"

"Okay," Jen croaked, and walked with Jack up to Brigid's bedroom.

12 — Limit

Jen let Jack lead her back up the stairs, past the old press on the first floor and up to Brigid's room. She was very aware of the size of him in a way that she hadn't been in years — aware of the callouses on his hands and the silver in his hair.

As they reached Brigid's room, both of them gazing down at that bed that had been the scene of so much magic over the past day, rather than up at the achingly lovely ceiling, a pulse of something passed through Jen — something lower than sound, brighter than light — and she gasped. "Brigid."

Jack squeezed her hand and nodded. His eyes showed concern but his brow was unfurrowed.

Another pulse of whatever it was passed through them, and Jen and Jack both shivered.

He murmured, "She's fine, sweetheart. Just blowing off some steam."

"Hell of a lot of tea," Jen tried to joke, but it she knew she sounded more concerned than amused.

"She'll be fine, Jen." Jack took her in his arms. "Brigid may not have the firmest grasp on what the rest of the world considers normal, but we have trust her to know her own needs. Her own limits. Just like we do with the kids."

Jen let her head fall against Jack's chest. "But she's not our child."

"No," Jack said. "She's not." Another pulse rippled up from the basement, making them both shudder. "Jen. This has changed everything. What we've done with Brigid."

She started to disagree, but then looked up into his eyes, and saw the concern and sincerity there: fundamental Jack Phalen. "Well, yeah. Having her back. Knowing what happened. It changes so much."

"True," said Jack slowly. "But not just that." He stroked her hair. "Making love with her — with both of you — was really amazing. All of those adolescent fantasies come to life. And I can honestly say now that I know that I'm married to the sexiest woman in the world, because here I've had mind-blowing sex with another girl that any man that liked women at all would give up his eyes to take to bed, and I've realized…" He pulled her to him, sighing into her hair. "All I want is you, sweetheart."

Jen wasn't sure which stunned her more: the statement or the raw feeling behind it. "I… But Jack…"

"I'm a simple guy, sweetheart. I've loved fucking Brigid, because she's wonderful, and beautiful, and because fucking a beautiful girl is nice. Unbelievable. And fucking her while she's eating your wife's pussy and your incredible wife is licking at your balls — it's fucking amazing. But it's not the same as what I have with you."

Jen, who had teased Jack for decades because he couldn't identify more than one feeling that he was experiencing at once, suddenly knew how he felt — knew what it meant to be so full of so many feelings that instead of being bands on a rainbow, they were a flurry of sparks, whirling too fast to follow, burning too hot to look at directly.

"Jen." Jack stepped back, his hands on her shoulders. "Jen, if you need us to move forward like this — with Brigid as part of the equation — or even if you need to… to be with Brigid instead of… I am happy to do it. I love you. I love Brigid, even if it's not the same. But I love you. And I can see how happy she makes you."

Tears overcame Jen, because honestly, she couldn't not cry. "God, Jack. It's not…" She burrowed back into his chest, felt him hesitate, but then wrap his arms around her. "You're my husband. You're the same man I've loved my whole adult life. I don't know what this is with Brigid. Honestly. But it doesn't change that."

He held her tight. When he spoke, his voice was thick. "Thank god. Because I… I wouldn't stand in your way, Jen, you know that, but it would…" Now he began to convulse within her arms. She could feel his throat working against the top of her head.

"Shh," she said, as much for herself as for him, and the two of them — neither of them much given to crying — stood at the foot of Brigid's bed and sobbed, clutching each other for dear life.

Eventually, together, they both began to settle. His breathing became regular. Her vision cleared, though her cheeks were still wet.

"When I came in to find the two of you… I was so angry about Tony, about Esau, and then the two of you —"

"Sorry," croaked Jen.

"For what?" He sounded both miserable and amused. "It was the sexiest fucking thing I've ever seen in my life."

"But it also made you wonder —"

" — if I was losing you. Yeah."

"Oh, Jack." She was desperately close to tears again, and she knew she couldn't do that to either of them. "Didn't think you'd get rid of me that easy, did you? Leave me in bed with our incredibly sexy, incredibly alive friend, and boom, you're rid of me?"

He snorted. "Damn. You figured out my dastardly plan."

"Pretty stupid plan, Jack. I win every which way."

"Oh, you do, do you?" He leaned back and smirked at her, face blotchy and wet, but a crooked smile in place.

"Yup. So here's your choice, Jack: are you staying on the winning side, or not?"

"Oh, I could never leave your side, so long as you let me stay." His smile softened, and then, as she'd hoped, he leaned back into her and gave her a long, warm, full-body kiss. The kind of kiss that can only come after fucking and fighting and children and years of being so close that you've forgotten. Not as pyrotechnic as their first kiss, or as desperate as the one she had given him all of those years ago on his birthday, or as electric as the one when they had finally made love, or the one the afternoon after the battle. This kiss was full of slow, deep fire, and they were just moths fluttering towards its light.

Eventually, he panted into her lips, "Jen. Do you think we could...?" One of his hands was up her shirt and on her breast, the other down the back of her pants. She was astonished to fill his cock pressing against her belly.

"Uh-huh." She was astonished that she had it in her to feel desire. But desire, apparently, was limited only by the flesh, and her flesh and spirit were both more than willing.

Without speaking any further, without parting any more than absolutely necessary, and without breaking that solar, immortal kiss, they divested themselves of clothing, lowered themselves to the bed, and Jack entered her — she took him in — and they made love.

The fuck was an extension of the kiss — not athletic or gymnastic, but slow and all-consuming.

"Oh, hell, Jack" Jen groaned, "I can't believe... you're still..."

"Told you," he panted into her ear, "you're all I need."

She laughed at the joy of it. "Don't need to bring you young virgins to deflower?"

"Nope," he groaned as she ran her fingers around his nipples. "'less you want to." His long fingers reached around her ass, his fingers sliding around his plowing cock and up her happily exhausted labia. "Just… want you."

And then they fell into the fuck — the endless, eternal fuck — and rolled themselves to timeless ecstasy there on Brigid's bed.

As they lay, gasping, wrapped in each other, still kissing, a small almost-animal whine came from the floor to the side of the bed.

Brigid sat in a patch of sunlight, leaning against the cupboard doors, her skirt up over her hips, her top up over her breasts. Her fingers were buried in her glistening pussy. She gave the whine again and shuddered, her eyelids fluttering closed. "That was even more beautiful than I thought it would be."

"Brigid." Jen was beyond shock. Certainly beyond shame. Mostly, in the moment, she was aware that Brigid had burned off one of her eyebrows, that the knuckles between her thighs looked fucking, and that her always-flyaway hair was looking distinctly knotted and scorched.

"Better?" rumbled Jack.

"Much," said Brigid, a tremor passing through her. "I broke some things that I shall probably regret breaking, and cast some rather inadvisable spells, but then I came up here, and saw something that I have dreamed about so many times, and it was just as it should have been, only more so."

"You could have joined us," Jack said. He was softening within her, but Jen found that she didn't want to let him go.

"Thank you, Jack. And I look forward to doing so again soon. However, my vaginal entrance is quite sore, and I think that between all of the wonderful sex that you both have given me and my rather considerable grief I don't know that even masturbating while watching you was a very good idea." She removed her fingers with a slurp, wincing before her expression returned to its usual blissful state.

"You're always welcome, Brigid, sweetheart," sighed Jen, feeling her cunt slowly, tragically pushing Jack out.

"Thank you, Jennifer." Brigid smiled, and it was truly blinding. "And I will. But seeing the two of you fucking reminded me of why I had always wanted to see you: because you fit. You are perfect. I am so glad that I was finally able to see you as you should be."

With a start, Jen realized that — even before they'd found Brigid — all of the sex of the past twenty-four hours or so had been one or the other of them pretending to be Brigid. Or Jack, with Brigid. But that Jen and her husband had never just... fucked.

And as amazing as the tying up and the pretending had been — her with Jack, her with Brigid, her with both of them — none of it had been what she and Jack had just shared.

Brigid nodded as if she were reading Jen's mind. "I hope that I have the opportunity to fuck you both — each — many more times. I hope that we have a lot of sex, and that maybe I will come truly to believe that you love me —" She raised her eyebrows, widening her eyes and silencing Jen and Jack's protests. "I know, of course, that you love me. Yet I find that knowing it and believing it are maybe rather different things."

Jack nodded, and the movement caused his cock to slip out from Jen, and they both moaned at the loss.

Brigid's smile didn't falter. "I want what you have," she said simply. "It is quite wonderful for me to know — and truly to believe — that you love each other. It is even more wonderful to watch it, as I have now been privileged to do. Thank you."

Jen smiled back, her arms and legs still enfolding Jack. "Welcome." She found her eyes filling again, but this time she knew just which part of the rainbow these tears came from: pure joy.

• •

They showered again — easily, comfortably, no need left for titillation or exploration — healing Brigid's self-inflicted wounds, regrowing her eyebrow, and combing out her hair. Together they dressed, and prepared for Tommy and Gabe to arrive with the children and the other guests. Jen was going to step Outside over to her family's and ask her mother if she might provide some tea, since the larder at the O'Danan's was bare, but as she opened the door, she found her mother coming up the walk with six large, enchanted hampers floating behind her, and found that, naturally, Emi Kamiyama had assumed that a welcome feast was in the offing for Brigid, and so had prepared enough food for twice as many people as would actually be coming.

"God, Mom!" laughed Jen, "I won't even begin to ask how you made all of this — how are we going to eat it!"

Smiling her most pleased smile, Jen's mother said, "Well, I suppose you could invite the rest of the family. After all, we are all overjoyed at Brigid's return. Bobby and Morgaine have called and said they're coming back as quickly as they can. Your other brothers have all asked...." She pursed her lips — Jen noticing the wrinkles there more than usual because of the low angle of the autumn afternoon sunlight. "Though of course, only if Brigid feels up to it. I'm so happy to see you, Brigid, dear," said Jen's Mom, sending the various hampers to various strategic spots around the O'Danans' kitchen

When Jen turned to ask, Brigid's shining eyes were all the answer that she needed. The ethereal redhead wafted across the floor to the anything but ethereal Emi Kamiyama, threw her arms around the older woman, and simply said, "Thank you, Mrs. Kamiyama."

Voice and hands fluttery, Jen's Mom patted Brigid on the back. "You're very welcome, Brigid, dear. Now, where should should we put the lemon squash?"

· ·

And so nearly the whole clan descended at five o'clock — Cousin George and his husband Bernie arriving first, as usual (never late to a party), followed by Sibella (George's sister), her husband Peter, and their little Lucy, who would be starting the Mountain in another year, Uncle Kip, who was looking more like the youngest of her dad's siblings rather than the second oldest, and finally Jen's oldest brother Hank, Michelle, their son Tommy, arm in arm with his new fiancée, Sally Beauchamp.

Jen felt a fresh wave of joy and nostalgia wash through her, looking at the young couple — at their wonder and their joy at being, finally, engaged (something that everyone in the family had seen coming far longer than they had). But also it took Jen's breath away to watch them approach a thoroughly wider-eyed-even-than-usual Brigid, and to realize with a visceral start that the two were in fact a bit older than Brigid.

"Brigid," laughed Tommy, his hair a shade of turquoise that he hadn't warn since childhood, "it's so wonderful to see you again! I don't know if you remember —"

"You're Tommy Kamiyama," said Brigid, wonder creeping into her voice as it was so often on her face. "Of course. I saw you just... For me it was just last week that I saw you, only you were three. You have your father's face."

Jen watched a familiar, Hank-like smirk appear on that Kamiyama face. He flashed a glance over at his dad, who winked back. "Well, fortunately, I have my mom's eyes," finished Tommy, since that was the old family joke.

Brigid tilted her head and stared at Tommy's blonde, very non-Japanese mane. "Also her hair."

Sally gave what was (for her, at least) a loud laugh.

Tommy grinned. "Yeah. True. I... I remember putting ketchup in my hair to try and get it to look like *yours*."

"Oh," said Brigid, and Jen was begin to recognize the particular panicked expression that mean that she was teetering at the edge of a temporal chasm. Then Brigid blinked, the chasm closed, and the smile returned. "How nice."

"He's been telling me and Addie about you for years," said Sally.

"Addie?" Brigid frowned.

"Oh, is she not here yet?" Tommy asked, looking around.

Jen broke in, "She's coming down from school with Gabe and the kids. They should be here soon."

"Oh, great!" said Tommy.

"She's always been a huge fan of yours," added Sally. "She's read everything you wrote."

"You mean... the Cryptogram?" Brigid was now looking thoroughly confused, which wasn't something Jen had ever seen.

"No!" laughed Tommy. "Though I worked on those over at Jack and Jen's on rainy days a lot. You wrote those? They were *tough!*"

Jen smiled. Even after all of these years, the family had never been able to complete all of the *Inquirer's* brain-teasers.

"I wrote... most of the magazine, especially after the war," Brigid said.

"Well," said Sally, reaching out and touching Brigid's shoulder with those ridiculously fine fingers of hers, "of course you did. It was the thaumazoological articles that I meant. Addie's just taken over as the Summoning teacher at the Mountain."

"Oh." Brigid was looking more her astonished, everyday self. "And she read my articles."

"Oh, yeah," Tommy answered. "I'd seen them because of the puzzles and told her about them, and so when she was looking for a graduate-level project, she went and found them. She's based all of her research on them since we left school. She's working on —"

But Brigid never got to hear that Tommy and Sally's friend was working on a new edition of Brigid's favorite book, Professor Schuler's *The Art of Summoning*, because at that moment, the front door flew open and Gabe arrived with the children. *All* of the children. Eddie, Jon, and Cindy, of course. Bobby and Morgaine's Allison and Brendan, Peter's dark-skinned, black-haired twins Roxie and Freddy, Peter and Sibella's little Emi (or Mojo, as she preferred to be known), and Tommy's younger siblings Cassie and Lou.

At the back of the herd came two non-Kamiyamas — Gabe's wife Lyndsey and the famous Addie.

"Sorry, Mom!" called Eddie, who seemed to have grown another two inches. "When word got out that we were coming down, *everyone* wanted to come!"

"Sorry, sorry, Brigid," Gabe laughed, "but it was all I could do not to bring the entire student body."

"The entire student body?" Brigid's eyes grew to breathtaking proportions. "But... Why?"

The kids all blinked at her. It was, of course, Jonathon who said what needed to be said. "Because you're a legend. You fought in three of the most important battles of the war. And our parents — not just the family, but all of the grownups who were in the original resistance — they all talk about you. As a friend."

"A... a friend?" Brigid looked closer to tears than smiling.

The small sea of black heads — and a couple of blondes — nodded. Jon continued, "And of course, we've been hearing about you in Summoning too." At the back of the throng, Addie laughed. "So we've all known about you our whole lives. And yeah, we all wanted to meet you, but —" He turned back to his cousins and they all nodded to him. " — there's one of us that really wants to meet you more than anyone." Jonathon put his hands on his sister's shoulders and gently propelled her forward.

Jen recognized the look on her daughter's face; it was an expression that had stuck itself on her own face at the same age, every time a certain black-haired, black-eyed boy had crossed her path. Mingled joy, terror, and adulation.

Still looking close to tears, but smiling, Brigid held out her hand. "You must be Cynthia."

Cindy took Brigid's hand and nodded emphatically. Her cousins all laughed — they knew that Cynthia had been as starstruck by her namesake as any racing fan had been with Jen. Cynthia's native fierceness showed through however; she turned and silenced her army of cousins with a glare, and then turned back to Brigid, eyes aflame with pride. "Cynthia *Brigid* Phalen. And you're... Brigid O'Danan."

Brigid began to say something, but Jen knew she'd never manage: the floodgates were open and Cindy rattled on, "You fought with Mommy and Daddy at the Battle of the Hall of Mirrors and at both of the Battles of the Mountain and you saved Mommy's life — *twice.* And you helped start the resistance and you believed in Cacodaemons and Agathodaemons and Eudaemons, and I believe in them too, even if *other people* don't." She shot a glare at her oldest brother, who was managing to look fairly respectful for once. "And you were the Winter dorms and I am too, and you wrote lots of great puzzles and animal stories and... and... And even though a lot of people didn't think you could still be alive, Mommy and I always knew you were alive. Oh, and Daddy too," she added. *Noblesse oblige.* Then Cindy's eyes grew Brigid-large and her voice Brigid-soft. "I'm so glad you are back."

"I am too," said Brigid, and accepted a hug from her biggest, smallest fan.

The whole room burst into applause, and so only those standing closest — Cynthia's brothers, Sally, Tommy, and Jen — could hear Cynthia say, "But I didn't know you'd be so beautiful."

As Brigid hugged Cynthia, Eddie muttered, "No kidding! Damn. She's not attached or anything, right?"

"Eddie!" groaned Jon. "Jesus!"

"No," laughed their mother. "That lovely lady is also my *oldest friend* and a quarter-century your senior. You might want to try finding someone a bit closer to your age." *And I am* not *going to share my lover with my son, thank you very much.*

"Yeah, maybe," said Eddie with a wink, "but she sure held up well!"

"You think," said Jack, hugging his eldest from behind, "that I'd have dated just *anyone* while your gorgeous mother decided whether or not to grace me with her attentions?"

"You dated *that?*" Eddie gasped. "No way!"

Jack smiled. "Well, it was just the one date, really, but —" He smiled at her. " — it really should have been a lot more than that. Don't you think, Jen?"

"Yup," laughed Jen. "I thought so at the time, and I think so now. You made an adorable couple."

Eddie scowled back at his parents, knowing he was missing the joke, and not sure it was one he wasn't better off missing. Which Jen was quite sure that he was. Finally he shrugged. "Well, I'd better get in line if I ever want to meet her."

Each of the cousins greeted Brigid warmly, and she seemed to glow more and more as the receiving line wound its way down.

The last two in the line where Lyndsey and Addie, who seemed barely to be holding herself back from exploding.

Lyndsey simply threw her arms around Brigid, and began to weep copiously into her shoulder. Brigid smiled and patted Lyndsey vaguely on the back. Eventually, Gabe disentangled his wife from Brigid, and led her over toward the Emi Kamiyama Commemorative Buffet.

That left only young Addie, who was positively vibrating in her black the Mountain professor's robes — Jen wasn't used to seeing her nephew's friend in anything but outdoor gear, so it looked as if the young teacher were playing dress-up. "Hello, you won't have heard of me, I'm not a Phalen or a Kamiyama or —"

"You must be Addie," said Brigid, taking Addie's hand and striking her briefly speechless. "Tommy and Sally were telling me that you are a thaumazoologist."

Addie blinked and nodded, and then gave a shrug. "Wish they wouldn't call me that. *Addie.* Got sick of the nickname years ago." Still holding Brigid's hand, still staring at Brigid's staring eyes, she gave a nervous laugh.

Jen found herself frozen. On the one hand, she wanted to help with the introduction. On the other, she felt a sudden lump of ice forming in her gut, and couldn't for the life of her figure out why.

"Well," Brigid mused, "I should call you something that you will actually answer to. What's your given name?"

Addie groaned. "Adolfina." She made a face. "Other than Vickie and Tommy and my family people usually just call me by my last name."

"Last name?" Brigid seemed to be scanning Addie's face for it.

Addie licked her lips. "Didn't I say? Um. Sorry. It. Uh. Schuler."

Brigid became stiller than still. "Schuler."

Addie nodded. "And that's, see, I wanted to talk with you about some of your articles about Duh migration patterns —"

"Schuler," Brigid repeated.

"Yeah. See, I'm working with my dad on —"

"*The Art of Summoning.*"

"Um." Addie's cheeks were pinkening. Jen tried to remember if she'd ever seen the normally self-possessed young woman look so thrown. "Yeah. Family thing. My grandfather —"

"—was my teacher." Brigid was peering deep into Addie's eyes now. "I do not believe that I could call you *Schuler*. The image that name evokes for me is of quite an old man, and not a very pretty young woman in possesion of all of her fingers."

Addie swallowed. "Um. Thanks?"

"And you do not wish to be called *Addie* or *Adolfina*."

Addie shook her head.

"Would you answer to *Fina?*"

Addie gave a nervous laugh. Her hand was shaking in Brigid's. "Uh, sounds like an Italian restaurant."

"Ah, true." Brigid pursed her lips, and for a moment Jen felt sure that Brigid was about to lean forward and kiss Addie, but no: *"Dolf?"*

Addie laughed again, but it was delighted laugh. *"Dolf?"*

Brigid nodded, looking rather pleased.

"Brigid," answered the newly-christened Professor Dolf Schuler, her voice low and sincere as she continued to clutch Brigid's hand, "you can call me anything you want." Then she looked at Jen and Jack, Sally and Tommy, and her face turned bright red.

"Oh, good," sighed Brigid and now she did lean forward and kiss Dolf — on the cheek. She slid her arm through Dolf's and led her toward the food. "Now tell me about your research. I am certain that advances in the field —"

As they walked away, Addie — *Dolf* — looked over her should and shot a nervous smile at her friends. Tommy and Sally both laughed and gave her the thumbs-up signal.

"Wow," said Tommy. "I didn't expect that! I mean, did you know Brigid swung that way?"

His arms around Jen's waist, Jack answered, "I think she's been figuring some things out."

Tommy and Sally both laughed again, and followed after their friend and Brigid.

"It's going to be okay, sweetheart," Jack whispered in Jen's ear. "It's not like they're getting married and having kids or anything."

Jen shook off the shock and what she now recognized as jealousy that had petrified her. "But... I feel so *stupid*. I mean..."

"I know, sweetheart." He kissed her ear. "Brigid loves you. Loves us. But it's good for her to be around someone her own age."

"I'm her age! I'm..." But Jen was so many things that she couldn't even say another word.

"Jen. Think about what we all said. After you and I made love. Brigid wants what you and I have. For herself. Doesn't she deserve that?"

Crying, Jen nodded.

"And who knows when she'll find it. A day ago, Brigid didn't even know it was *possible* for two women to love each other that way. Let her figure things out." He kissed her neck and gave her a squeeze.

"Okay," sighed Jen, thinking that it was a bad joke to have to let go of a new-found lover just as she was having to let go of her children.

"In the mean time," Jack said into her ear in a manner that elicited responses that Jen honestly wouldn't have thought herself capable of, "we've told her she's always welcome in our bed, and she made it very clear that she plans on taking us up on that."

"Okay," sighed Jen again, much lower this time.

"Ew!" shouted Eddie from the other side of the room. "Gross! Parent smooching!"

There was a general laugh around the room. Jen flipped her eldest the bird, which evoked an even louder laugh.

And a delighted, delightful smile from a red-haired, emerald-eyed face that Jen had despaired ever to see again.

"Okay," repeated Jen once more, meaning it, turning in her husband's arms and kissing him soundly both for her son's benefit, and more particularly for her own.

It was of course at that precise moment that Emi and Kenji Kamiyama finally arrived, with Bobby and Morgaine in tow. "Sorry we're late! Kenji working too hard as usual! Look who called in just now! *JENNIFER... PHALEN!* What do you think — !"

Morgaine and Bobby escaped toward Brigid, waving wildly, Morgaine weeping.

"I believe, Emi dear, that she is kissing her husband," said Jen's dad, spinning his own spouse, dipping her, and smooching her to another round of cheers.

Once the hilarity had settled, and Bobby had separated an utterly discomposed Morgaine from Brigid, the evening turned into something like a regular Kamiyama Family Picnic — people swapping stories, kids playing jokes on each other and (more frequently) on the adults. Various parents hugging their children, the children desperately trying to break away.

The one difference was that the center of gravity of this party was clearly Brigid, and she was happier, basking in the combined love of the assembled extended clan, than Jen could ever remember seeing her. Well, except for a couple of occasions the previous night. And earlier that day. In bed.

It was really… difficult having all of those thoughts and memories so close to the surface at a family do.

And it was very confusing to watch Addie's — Dolf's — bright infatuation, which Brigid seemed to be reveling in, and *not* feel jealous.

Too soon, Gabe called out, "It's almost curfew." There was a groan from the younger members of the party. "Yes, yes, I know we would all love to stay, but the agreement that I made with you and with the chancellor was to return to school before the curfew bell rang. Do we want her to be glad that he allowed us to come and celebrate with Brigid, or do we want her to regret it?"

"Glad," grumbled most of the kids. Eddie, naturally, grumbled something unrepeatable, earning him suitably disapproving glares from both of his parents — who had just put that particular unrepeatable word into practice more often over the previous day than they could ever remember doing.

All of the kids went to say goodbye to their parents and siblings. Jen and Jack hugged each of their kids in turn; as soon as Cindy had received her parental blessing, however, she ran over to Brigid, who was talking to Hank and Sally, and stuck out her hand. "It's a pleasure to meet you, Ms. O'Danan."

Brigid gathered Jen's gangly eleven-year-old daughter up in her arms and hugged her. "It is a pleasure to meet you as well, Cynthia. And you must call me Brigid, please. I shall write to you, if I may."

Cindy's face shone. "Oh, *please!*" she said, throwing her arms around Brigid's neck and kissing her cheek. "Bye! Bye, Mommy, bye Daddy! Bye everyone!" And she followed the rest of the kids outside.

"Professor Schuler," called Gabe as he scooted all of the kids out the door, "will you be returning with us?"

Dolf (it was going to take some getting used to, calling her that — even harder than thinking of *Professor Schuler* as someone young, pretty, and dressed in jeans and t-sirts) blinked at Sally and Tommy, who were talking with Uncle Kip, and then to Brigid, who gave her a warm smile. "Um, would you mind if I found my own way back? I don't have rounds until Sunday night."

Gabe smiled back at her. "Of course not. Goodbye, everyone! Welcome home, Brigid."

The party began to break up after that. Jen's dad was exhausted after a long week, and her mother wanted to make sure that her husband could step Outside without incident. (Jen suspected more smooching was on the agenda, but didn't particular care to ask.) Bobby and Morgaine, who had traveled back from Argentina as soon as they heard about Brigid's return, needed to get back to the conference — and their second honeymoon. Peter and Sibella needed to get Lucy to bed (much to her loud disgust), and George and Bernie, Hank and Michelle were all off to catch the end of a broadcast of a mundane basketball game— Michelle had always loved the game, and so far had managed to share it with Uncle George and his husband — Michelle giggled something that sounded as if it were about the fit of the players' uniforms. And Hank, of course, enjoyed anything that Michelle enjoyed.

That left Jen and Jack, Brigid, Kip, Sally, Tommy, and Dolf, and they all cleaned up together, even as Brigid, Kip, and Dolf shared stories about dragons and other beasties.

Once the kitchen was once again clean, Kip suggested that they all go down to the Wyvern, where there was usually a band and always good beer. Sally, Tommy, and Dolf all quickly agreed

Jack shook his head, and Jen found herself agreeing. It had been a long, long, eventful day and a half.

"Come with us, Brigid," Dolf said, "we can dance."

Jen found herself staring at Brigid, who was standing undecided, found herself thinking, *Don't leave me. Please don't leave me.* And angry to be thinking such things.

"I don't like dancing, actually." Brigid smiled back at Jen, and then turned to Dolf. "I'll join you at the Wyvern in a few minutes. I should like some time with Jack and Jen."

The young contingent took this at face value, Dolf looking very happy — and Jen couldn't help but be happy for her. Kip raised an eyebrow. "Go, Charles," Brigid said, "Jen and Jack are my best friends, and they brought me back to life, and I feel as if I really should thank them properly."

Kip gave his usual gruff laugh, and walked to the door. "Bye, Jen,

Jack! See you at the Wyvern, Brigid."

As soon as Kip closed the door, Brigid sprinted to Jen and Jack — moving more quickly than Jen could remember her doing except in combat. She threw her hands around them both. "I love you, Jen. I love you, Jack."

"Love you," Jen and her husband muttered into the hug.

"I think," whispered Brigid, "that Dolf finds me attractive."

Jen laughed. "I think you're fucking well right!"

"I think that she is a... a lesbite?"

"Lesbian," Jack said, stroking Brigid's hair. "Yeah. She is."

"Hmm." Brigid rested her head in the crevice between Jack's chest and Jen's breasts. "I have been thinking very hard about what we discussed this afternoon."

"Brigid," Jen found herself saying, "Addie — Dolf is a wonderful girl. We've known her for... for years. And she clearly *really* likes you."

"You think so?" came the muffled question.

"Yeah," chuckled Jack, stroking Jen's hair and Brigid's both, now. "We think so."

Jen looked her husband in the eye, looking for his strength. "We love you, Brigid. We will always love you. But you have a chance to find someone who's just yours..."

Brigid lifted her head. "Thank you." She kissed Jen on the lips, and whispered into them, "You will always be my very best friend, Jennifer. Always." She kissed Jack on the lips and said, "And you will always be my Jack. You will always be my first, and I will always treasure that."

Jack's grimace of a smile reflected the conflict in Jen's heart. "Go. We won't wait up."

Brigid smiled brilliantly. "I do love you both." She skipped toward the door and then turned back. "You know, it occurs to me, I do not know if a romantic relationship between myself and Dolf is likely to establish itself very quickly, if at all. She will be teaching. Until such time, would the two of you mind allowing me to join you in bed so that we can all fuck some more?"

Jack coughed, but Jen had seen this coming. "We'd love that, Brigid. You are always welcome in our bed."

"Oh." Brigid glowed, and Jen could make out the ghost of those amazing nipples through her top. "Thank you. I love you both very much." And with that, Brigid O'Danan opened the door and left her home for the first time in twenty years.

Jen and Jack stood there, both looking at the door, until long after the *pop* of Brigid's Apparition had faded.

At last, Jen squeezed Jack's hand. "Come on, sweetie," she said. "Let's go up to sleep."

He leaned in and kissed her, and her body could feel the echo of that wonderful, amazing, astonishing kiss from that afternoon. "To sleep."

Epilogue — Infinity

"God, Mom, cut it out!" laughed Cynthia, her grin a rictus of exasperation. "Go already. I'm sixteen, not six. And it's not like I'm going to blow the house up, like Eddie might have, or invite all my pals, like Al!"

Sighing, Jen looked up at her daughter, who'd shot up another two inches since the beginning of the school year. Babies... "We wouldn't have left them alone at all," she said, and smoothed her daughter's hair back off of her face.

When Cynthia shook the hair defiantly back into her face, Jack laughed, the traitorous bastard, and said, "In any case, we know our girl. You just want to tuck into your Christmas books."

Cynthia shot him a smirk — funny how Jen always got the vexation while Jack always got the grin — and hugged them both. "Wish I could go with you."

"Brigid and Dolf had something they wanted to ask us about," said Jack with a very parental shrug.

"Besides," said Jen, jumping in, "you get to see them all of the time at school. We haven't had a chance actually to spend time with them since Brigid's birthday." Her twenty-fifth/forty-fifth. Fifth anniversary of her and Dolf meeting. Second anniversary of their wedding...

"Though why those two would want to spend time with a boring old pair like you two, God only knows."

Jack poked Cynthia in the ribs, setting off a predictable squeal of laughter. Cynthia grabbed her father's finger before he could attack again, and her face took on a quizzical seriousness. "Daddy? Did you really, you know, date Brigid?"

Jack shrugged.

"I mean," said Cynthia, "she and Dolfie seem so happy, you know? It's hard to think of her dating —" Jack raised an eyebrow and she ducked her head. "I mean, not dating you, just… You know. A guy."

Jen leaned forward and kissed Cynthia on the cheek. "It's not as if it's an either/or thing, you know." *Not as if anything with Brigid is that simple.*

"'Course." Cynthia nodded seriously and then smiled, hugging her parents. "Give Brigid and Dolfie my love!"

As Jen and Jack walked out into the slushy Sunrise Valley, he murmured to her, "Why the fascination with Brigid's love life?"

Jen shrugged. "Cynthia's always been a bit obsessed with Brigid."

"Yeah," said Jack, scowling. "I guess… I don't want Cynthia thinking she should be interested in girls — or boys, or both — just because Brigid is."

Jen squeezed his hand. "Do you really think our daughter would do anything she didn't want to?"

Jack smiled at that. "No. I guess not."

"Besides," Jen whispered in his ear, "her mother is interested in girls because Brigid is. Well. Is interested in Brigid, anyway."

He shivered and turned, kissing her. "You still okay with that? She hasn't… been with us in a while. Last winter."

"Jack," she sighed into his neck. "God, I'm a lucky witch. A gorgeous younger woman stops hopping into our bed and my husband's worried about *me.*"

"You know you're enough for me."

"As you are for me, sweetheart." She kissed his chin. "Come on. Let's go see what the love birds want."

• •

It was as always an eerie pleasure to walk into the re-vivified, re-messified O'Danan house. Brigid's home was Brigid's once more — cluttered, chaotic — and the twenty-year sterile, tidy span existed now only in Jen's memory.

"Jack! Jen!" Brigid wafted over to them from the oven, which seemed to be emitting lavender smoke. "It's lovely to see you." As always, she kissed each of them warmly on the lips. Even as the kiss warmed Jen, it made her uncomfortable. She knew it made Jack uncomfortable. She assumed it made Dolf uncomfortable.

And yet none of them seemed capable of asking Brigid to stop.

As they shed their coats — valley sleet had given way to snow up here in the hills — Jack asked, "Where's Dolf?"

"Oh," sighed Brigid, meandering back toward the oven. "She wanted to get changed." With a vague flick of her wand, Brigid opened the oven door, revealing a beautiful roast... something. Jen wasn't sure she wanted to know what species the meat was from, but it smelled delicious.

"Was she up with her beasties today?" Jack asked, nostrils flaring.

"Hmm?" Brigid cocked her head, leaving the roast floating in mid-air. "No. We've been home all day." With a nod, Brigid finished transporting the roasting pan to the counter.

"Changed?" Jack asked.

That didn't sound like Dolf at all. As long as they'd known Addie Schuler, she'd never dressed up of her own volition, preferring work clothes and boots to dresses. "I hope she's not getting done up on our account!" Jen laughed.

Brigid turned to them once more, smiling. "Well, of course... Oh." Her eyes flew disconcertingly wide. "Oh, dear. I've done it again. I've forgot to tell you why we've asked you." Brigid's face took on what was for her a pensive expression. "I suppose I should wait for Dolf to be here before we discuss it."

"All right," Jen laughed, giddy even now that the wonder that was Brigid had been returned to her — to all of them. "Need some help with the roast?"

"Oh, no, thank you," Brigid sighed, undoing the button to her blouse. A green jewel caught the light.

"Is that... your choker?" Jack asked.

"Hmm?" Brigid touched it with one long finger. "Oh. Yes."

Jack's eyebrows flew up into his hairline and he caught Jen's eye.

What the hell? Brigid had always worn the choker — and the incredibly naughty nightie — when she had joined Jen and Jack in bed. Jen hadn't ever seen her friend put it on for any other occasion. It had been almost a year, and though Dolf knew... Why...?

"Oh, Dolf," sighed Brigid, "don't you look lovely."

Down the staircase came Dolf — Adolfina Schuler — very lovely indeed in a midnight blue silk dress that clung to her body in a manner that Jen knew that even Jack would notice.

Like Brigid, Dolf was a beautiful young woman. Like Brigid, she wore her beauty carelessly, without any apparent awareness or effort.

It was part of their charm, as women and as a couple. Yet there was nothing negligent about Dolf's appearance tonight. She was dressed to *kill*.

She was also looking supremely self-conscious, her eyes downcast in a way that Jen couldn't remember them ever being before.

Seeing her husband's mouth wide open, Jen laughed in spite of her own growing uncertainty. "You do, Dolf. You look gorgeous." Jack nodded. "Cynthia sends you both her love, by the way."

Now the familiar spark lit Dolf's face and her eyes flashed up. "She's amazing. Has she told you about the Cockatrice-breeding project that she's been helping me with?"

And that launched them into a wonderful and almost normal dinner — at least, as normal as dinner with Brigid and her wife could or should ever be.

It didn't stop flutters of anxiety from passing around the table — to everyone except Brigid, of course. Jen wasn't sure what the two girls — women — were up to, but she was fairly certain that a nice meal wasn't the end of it.

As they washed down a wonderful chocolate torte with a lovely raspberry-tinged ale, Jen finally asked, "So, ladies. What was it you wanted to talk to us about?"

Alarm flared in Dolf's eyes, but Brigid took her wife's hand and smiled, calm as ever. "Yes, dear, I apparently forgot to tell them, but I know that they won't mind."

"Mind?" asked Jack, putting down his glass.

"Well, yes," said Brigid with a broad smile, "I don't think you'll mind, you see, because it involves sex, which I know that you both enjoy as much as we do."

Dolf and Jack suddenly both looked as if they wanted to hide beneath the table.

"Sex?" Jen asked, willing her breath to remain even.

"Well, yes," Brigid agreed, looking pleased with herself. "Since Dolf and I both want to get pregnant, you see, that seemed like the best way about it."

"Sex?" Jack asked.

"Pregnant?" asked Jen. "*Both?*"

"Oh, yes," said Brigid, opening her blouse further to reveal that beneath them she was wearing only the magical emerald green silk negligee. "You see, we both rather love babies, and we both rather want them, and while Dolf has never been with a man, she is quite fond of Jack and, of course, she has always found you desperately attractive, Jen."

"Me?"

Dolf's face was bright red, but her eyes bored into Jen's. "That's, um, why I've never felt jealous when Bri, um, joined you guys. Envious, I guess, a bit, but… I thought she'd talked to you about this, but I guess she's been off Cacodaemon hunting…?"

Brigid nodded, smiling.

Dolf's eyes flashed first to her wife, then back to Jen, and then to Jack. "And… Bri's told me about… that first time with you, Jack. And… with both of you, how you, um, helped, Jen, and honestly, Bri made it sound like the sexiest fucking thing ever, but then everything about Bri is the sexiest fucking thing ever, you know?"

Jen looked at Brigid, half-dressed, licking chocolate off of her finger, and couldn't help but nod in agreement.

In Dolf's dark blue dress, a tiny half-moon of darker shadow revealed a nipple rising beneath the silk on each breast. Her eyes still on Jen, Dolf reached across and took Jack's hand. "Would you do that for me, Jen? Jack? Would you do for me… what you did for Brigid?"

Jack licked his lips. With his free hand, he took Jen's. "I'd be honored."

Brigid reached out, taking Jen's other hand, and Dolf's. "And you, Jen? Will you fuck my beautiful wife with your husband? And me, of course, since we're both ovulating?"

Heart beating in her throat, Jen nodded.

(Babies…)

Brigid stood, releasing their hands and letting her blouse fall to reveal the marble-white body that did such unforeseeable things to Jen's heart, and to the rest of her body.

"Oh, good," Brigid said, leading the other three away from the table and toward the stairs. "I've enlarged the bed. I've been thinking of some ways for the four of us to enjoy each other that I think you will all find quite interesting."

She stopped at the base of the stairs and turned to the other three. "You brought me back to life here, Jen and Jack. You changed my life here, Dolf. It seems appropriate that it will have been the place where we kindled new lives as well, don't you think?"

When Jen, Jack, and Dolf all nodded mutely, she smiled, turned again, and walked up the stairs, silk-draped ass swaying in negligent seduction, leading them up and on into the future.

• •

When James and Joseph were born, their eyes were black-on-black.

Mind, body, and heart full, Jen wasn't at all surprised to find that she loved them as if they were her own.

~FIN~

Dear Reader,

Thanks so much for taking the time to read Jen's story of discovery and rediscovery.

If you enjoyed *By the Numbers*, please consider telling your friends or posting a short, honest review. Word of mouth is an author's best friend — and I'd like to think you'd be doing your friends a favor. You can leave a review at Stillpoint/Eros (stilpt.us/by-the-numbers?review), at Goodreads (stilpt.us/by-the-numbers?goodreads), or, if you'd prefer, at Amazon (stilpt.us/by-the-numbers?amazon). And of course, anywhere else you'd like.

If you do post a review — glowing or not — and send Stillpoint/Eros a screenshot or link, and they'll send you a download coupon good for any of their books — as well as free download code good at the world's largest audiobook library, Audible.com.*

If you'd like to contact me directly, or you have any questions for me, my email is kdwest@stillpointdigital.com. I'm also on social media; see below for where to find me. I'd love to hear from you.

Until next time!

K.D. West

Blog: kdwestwrites.wordpress.com
Publisher page: stillpointeros.com/kdwest
Facebook Author Page: facebook.com/kdwestauthor
Twitter: @kdwestwrites
Google+: plus.google.com/+kdwest
Pinterest: kdwestwrites.pinterest.com
Tumblr: kdwestwrites.tumblr.com

---

* While supplies last, of course!

Sneak Peek:
The Visitor Arrives
A Tale of Embracing the Unknown... Literally

Lea didn't usually masturbate in airplane bathrooms, because, after all, they're bathrooms. On airplanes.

But half of the way through the long flight across the country to Atlanta, she found herself in the tiny, tinny cubicle with one foot up on the wall and the other in the sink, with her fingers buried to the second knuckle in her pussy.

Thinking of Sean, her best friend's older brother.

Sean the firefighter of the broad shoulders and the narrow hips. Sean of the gentle Southern drawl, the polite tone, the blue eyes, and the wicked, square-jawed smile.

Sean, who she had always wanted to wrap her arms and legs around, but never managed to do more than flirt with a bit.

Sean. Who had found out that she was interviewing for the job in Atlanta and had, with smooth, apparently subtext-less Southern hospitality, invited her to save the cost of a hotel room and stay with him. Well, on the sofa of the apartment he shared. But still. Just a door away... *Oooo*, Sean.

She wanted him. She had always wanted him, since she was a college sophomore and his sister Kirsten's roomie. She wanted his strong arms around her. Wanted his big hands pulling her pelvis tight against his. Wanted to feel what she knew would be his big, thick cock spreading... *Ooo...!*

With a shudder of pleasure and relief that she knew was only temporary, she came, swallowing as best she could the groan that wanted to explode from her gut.

Carefully, quickly, Lea lowered her legs, pulled up her panties, pulled down her skirt and smoothed it as best she could, washed her hands, and opened the bathroom door.

A woman just a few years older than Lea stood in the narrow galley glaring daggers at her. Her elbow-high child was doing a dance that made unmistakably clear just how long they'd had to wait.

"Sorry," Lea murmured. "Thanks."

"Yaw're welcome," the mother grumbled in a thick-as-honey accent that made Lea feel anything but welcome as the woman and her child pushed past.

Even so, hearing that Southern sound got Lea thinking of Sean again, of his arms and chest and ass and mouth… and got her wondering just how long the mom and kid were going to take, because, oh, she could have started all over, airplane bathroom or no.

• •

The plane finally landed and Lea picked up the beat-up old Civic she'd rented. Sean had told her that he'd have loved to pick her up, but he wasn't going to be getting off duty until about the time Lea landed, and since she was going to need a car the next day anyway to get to the interview, she drove herself north from the airport — around the city and into Cobb County, where Sean and the other firefighter shared a place, where she'd be sleeping on their couch.

Well, she thought let's not lie: Lea hoped that she wouldn't be sleeping on their couch. She hoped very much that she would at last be sharing Sean's bed. She knew that she should have been thinking about the interview, but hey — there are lots of jobs. There was only one Sean, and she'd lusted after him for far too long.

Well. She was thinking about the job interview. It was for the position of assistant business manager of a mid-sized professional theater — her chance finally to work somewhere other than the glorified community theaters she'd been slaving at since graduation. She was excited by the opportunity.

But Sean….

Her thoughts less on the road than they should have been, she followed her phone's directions around the city, past dozens of malls, hotels, and office buildings mostly bearing the name Peachtree Whatever, and out into the gently rolling hills and lush greenery of the Atlanta suburbs. "Exit the highway," said her phone, and she exited. "Turn left," it intoned, and she turned left.

She wondered if she could give her GPS voice a Southern accent. *Tuhn leyeft, honey.* That thought made Lea smile.

She reached the complex, parked, and followed Sean's very clear directions to his second-floor apartment. Fighting down the images of Sean's broad chest — and narrow hips — that had driven her to the airplane lavatory, she knocked on the door.

A muffled voice called out, "C'me in! It's unlocked."

She opened the door and was assaulted simultaneously by the delicious smells of something sweet baking and something frying, as well as by the vision of the tall, tapered figure at the stove.

Him. Cooking. Looking like every masturbatory fantasy Lea had ever had about him, only better. Except fully dressed, but food. *Shit.*

"Sorry I couldn't come to the door," he said in that sweet Georgia drawl. He finished flipping something in the pan. "I'm up to my elbows in fried chicken. Hope you like —"

Lea threw her arms around him from behind and took joy in squeezing his chest hard. "I love it! Thank you so much for having me."

"Uh. Welcome." He stiffened before relaxing and turning in her grasp. "Nice to meet you, too, miss."

Lea looked up at the eyes smiling down at her. Brown. At the dimpled chin. Not Sean. Oh, SHIT. She released the man — he had to be Sean's roomie — and stammered, "I'm so, so... I, uh..."

"Naw, miss, don't be sorry, that was a nice hello, no doubt!" The roommate put down his tongs and smiled at her. He held out his enormous hand. "I'm Andrew. You must be Lea."

She shook his hand and nodded, still speechless.

His grin grew. "Really, don't feel bad. It happens more often than you'd think — the captain mixes us up so much he's taken to just calling us the Twins."

"Huh," Lea grunted. She was feeling the ghost of that muscled chest on her fingers.

"There you are, Lea!" Another Southern voice called from the other side of the apartment. She turned: it was Sean, no doubt this time. Blue eyes. Square jaw. Nothing on but a towel around his waist. Oh. Shitty shit-shit. He ran his hand through his short, wet hair. "Sorry, I was just taking a shower, I didn't want you to have to smell me like the hog I am."

"Huh," Lea repeated.

Sean smiled warmly. "I see you met Andy. I hope, Andy," he said, his voice lowering in mock threat, "that you've conducted yourself like a gentleman toward this young lady."

"I wasn't the one came out half-naked," joked Andy.

Lea found her voice. "Besides, I was the one molesting him."

Sean raised his eyebrow, that supremely wicked grin on display.

"Yeah," laughed Andy, "lucky me! She thought I was you. Couldn't see your ugly face 'cause I was dealing with supper."

"My ugly face!"

"Anyhow," Andy laughed, "why didn't you tell me our visitor was such a bombshell? Begging your pardon, Miss Lea."

Lea felt Sean's eyes flash to hers, saw the smile turn from wicked to evil. "Didn't want you getting ideas, Andy."

Lea couldn't think of anything to say to that.

"Ideas, huh?" Andy snorted and turned back to the stove. "You go get some pants on, boy, and we'll have some supper and then we can talk about who's getting ideas."

Now Sean's grin turned sunny again; he waved and turned, and Lea was treated to the sight of his retreating, naked, rippling back and his tight, towel-clad ass as they made their way down the hall.

I'm getting ideas, Lea thought, and then tried very hard not to think any more.

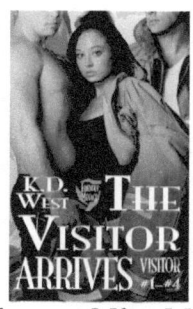

It's the the world's oldest story:
A girl, her fireman, and her other fireman.

When Lea heads off to Atlanta for a job interview, all she's thinking about is the work. Well, and Sean, her best friend's brother. Sean, the tall, muscular firefighter. With the gentle Southern drawl and the wicked smile. Whose couch she's going to be sleeping on.

Well, actually, whose couch she hopes very much she won't be sleeping on. But it turns out that Andy, Sean's roommate, is another, equally hot Southern firefighter, and so when a visitor — or perhaps two — joins Lea on that couch, it sparks a series of events that none of them could possibly have foreseen.

But that none of them regrets. Not even a little bit.

This collection contains the first four installments in The Visitor Saga:
1. The Visitor
2. The Visitor Comes Home
3. The Visitor Comes Again
4. The Visitor Goes to Work

Also available
The exciting conclusion to the series

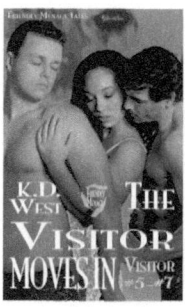

StillpointEros.com/VisitorSaga

About K.D. West

The Amazon best-selling author of the *Erotic Tales: Letters to Allison* and *Juliet Takes Flight* story cycles as well as the up-coming novel *A Joy Forever: An Erotic Education*, **K.D. West** is a teacher, writer and performer living in a small suburb of a big city:

> Not a huge amount to say — I'm an author of steamy stories who happens to be a teacher; these things don't mix well in public, so I tend to be fairly quiet about real life in my blogging. I am, however, interested in all sorts of things — books, writing, theater, mythology, and, obviously, erotica! I'm a huge reader of genre fiction — mostly mysteries and fantasy, but also science fiction and historical romance.

West is working on two intertwined series involving a young woman and her older lover (the *Juliet Takes Flight* and *Erotic Tales: Letters to Allison* stories), a series of stories about friends discovering that they can become much more (*Friendly Ménage Tales*), and a series of the kinds of fairytales that the Brothers Grimm might have written if they'd been interested in stories where the heroine got the princess (*Sapphic Fairytales*).

By the Numbers is K.D. West's first novel.